ANGELS OF STOCKHOLM

Angels of Stockholm

Stories

by

NEIL D. DESMOND

Adelaide Books
New York/Lisbon
2018

ANGELS OF STOCKHOLM
Stories
By Neil D. Desmond

Copyright © by Neil D. Desmond

Cover design © 2018 Adelaide Books

Published by Adelaide Books, New York / Lisbon
adelaidebooks.org

Editor-in-Chief
Stevan V. Nikolic

For any information, please address Adelaide Books
at info@adelaidebooks.org

or write to:

Adelaide Books
244 Fifth Ave. Suite D27
New York, NY, 10001

ISBN-13: 978-1-949180-54-1

ISBN-10: 1-949180-54-9

Printed in the United States of America

Contents

Angels of Stockholm

Hans' sister was to his right and his six year old son, Peter, was to his left as he sat and listened to the sermon. The pastor of St. Lucia's Catholic Church, in downtown Stockholm, was reading from the Gospel According to John on this Sunday morning in the spring of 1945. Hans, however, was trying to get Peter to stop fidgeting and pay attention. "What are you doing? Why aren't you listening? I thought you were going to pay attention this time."

Peter looked up at his father. Peter had become distant and withdrawn since the sudden passing of his mother more than two years earlier.

"You did not choose me, I chose you…" the Pastor continued, quoting Jesus.

"I am listening," Peter claimed. Hans was skeptical.

"Well, what did the Pastor say, then?" Hans wanted to know, his eyebrow raised at the boy.

"He said Jesus chooses us, not the other way around…" the boy replied.

Hans believed that Peter was indeed, chosen. He realized it when he saw how Peter behaved around pets and younger children. Peter seemed to love things smaller and weaker than he was. Hans believed that was a sign of divinity. Conversely, those whose allegiance was to the bigger and stronger were depraved. There was something wrong with them, Hans believed.

The Pastor's words came in and out for Hans, like a radio station with intermittent static. He had to keep an eye on Peter, much more so than when his wife was alive. The Pastor had moved away from the Scripture itself, and was now connecting it to everyday life. "We don't choose responsibilities in life," he said. "Responsibilities choose us." Hans did hear that statement. At that moment, he turned his attention away from the child and toward the Pastor, his eye brow still raised.

MAUTHAUSEN, AUSTRIA

Marina cut her small ration in half, sharing with the sick (possibly dying) young girl she had been trying to look after. The girl was too weak to leave the cramped, dirty sleeping quarters to work in the camp. Marina feared the girl would be sent to the gas chamber if the guards deemed her incapable of labor. Marina was beginning to think this might be worse than Auschwitz, where she and many other women and children had come from in the fall of 1944. She had hoped the transfer would have improved her chances of survival, but it appeared now there wasn't much difference between one labor camp or another. Hope was in short supply, but not totally eradicated. Marina had heard rumors recently in the camp. Rumors the war was ending and the allies had won. Rumors of liberation. But she, like the other prisoners, had heard about liberators coming to save their lives before and it never seemed to happen. First they were coming from the East by rail. Then they were coming from the West in tanks. Then they were coming from the South by rail. The latest rumor concerned liberators from North. They would arrive, the rumors had it, in white buses. Hope springs eternal, Marina supposed. What had happened to her and the other prisoners over the last few years was so incomprehensible, even those in the camps were searching for some existential narrative that made sense. What had been happening simply wasn't possible, yet it was happening.

Marina was from a small town outside of Warsaw. She was thirty one years old and had been in the camps for four and half years. Her husband died at Auschwitz. She had not seen or heard from her daughter, who would now be nine years old, since her internment. She did not know if her daughter was alive or dead. She feared the worst.

One of the other female prisoners entered the barracks and looked over the sick girl. She shook her head and took a deep breath, before turning her attention to Marina. "So this time they're coming from Sweden to save us, are they?" her voice tinged with sarcasm. Marina looked back at the woman, unsure how she felt about the woman's attitude. "Like angels swooping down from above to carry us all away? Is that the story?" the woman continued, smirking at Marina.

One of the ways Marina dealt with the separation from her daughter was by looking after the children in the camp. She once persuaded a guard (at risk to her own life) not to shoot a fourteen year old boy who had accidentally broken a tool in the machine shop. But if bullets didn't get these children, Marina knew, hunger and illness would. Almost all of them were sick and weak by the spring of 1945. Marina had seen many people die in the camps. Rumors aside, she believed most of the prisoners at Mauthausen would soon meet their end, including herself. She believed she would die in this damp and ugly place.

STOCKHOLM

Hans' sister took Peter back to the family home (Hans had moved back home after his wife's death) and Hans walked from the church to Stockholm's Central Bus Terminal. He was meeting individually with his boss, for reasons not yet clear to him. Hans was thirty four years old and had been driving for the city transit authority for nine years. He was regarded as one of, if not the, safest bus driver in the city. He had never caused an accident, and usually won the skills competitions the Authority held every so often.

"So, why did you call me in here on a Sunday? What do we need to talk about that couldn't wait until tomorrow?" Hans wondered aloud as his boss, Erik, sat across from him at his desk.

"We need a number of drivers, hopefully thirty or forty, for a special assignment," Erik replied.

"A special assignment? Alright, I'm listening," Hans said, folding his hands on his lap.

"We need drivers to go into Austria, driving those ambulatory buses from the Red Cross, you can handle one of those, right?"

Hans scoffed at the question, "Of course I can handle one of those," he replied.

"I figured so, you're the best we've got," Erik continued. "Anyway, I say Austria because we are hoping to bring hundreds of refugees to Sweden. We have learned many refugees are there, women and children, and they are sick. They can't go back where they came from, at least not at this time."

Both Erik and Hans were under the mistaken impression the camps were "refugee camps" as opposed to the concentration camps they were. "It is a dangerous assignment," Erik continued. "There may be land mines on the way. There may be rogue Nazi elements along the road. We can't guarantee your safety. But I am hoping you will consider this, Hans. We've had only six volunteers so far. I have some documents for you to look over and, if you decide to go, sign."

Hans was taken aback by what was being proposed. "Look, I have a young boy at home. I'm his only parent. His mother died of a brain hemorrhage…" Erik's phone started ringing, interrupting Hans in mid-sentence.

"Let me get that, it might be important," Erik said. He picked up the phone and began a conversation which Hans found difficult to follow from the other side of the desk. Hans' eyes started wandering around the office as the call lasted longer than either of them had expected. Hans noticed a document to his right, at the edge of the desk. He began reading it upside down and realized it was a list of names, names he recognized.

Ariel Fischler

Yusef Fink

Joel Ginsburg

David Rhienquest

Norman Lowenstein

Benjamin Rubenstein

Erik hung up the phone without saying goodbye and seemed angry at whoever was at the other end. "Sorry," he resumed. "As I was saying, Hans, this is a dangerous…"

"What's that list?" Hans inquired, interrupting and nodding to his right.

Erik looked to his left and picked up the list of names. "Oh, this is the list of guys who have volunteered for this assignment," he replied.

"I know all of those guys," Hans stated. "They're all Jewish."

Erik leaned back in his chair. He seemed taken aback by Hans' observation. He looked over the list again. "Okay, I suppose they are." Erik put down the list and looked at Hans. The two made eye contact.

"You mean to tell me no Christian drivers have signed up for this assignment yet?" Hans asked, holding the eye contact.

"Well, not yet, no," Erik replied, somewhat clumsily. He was puzzled by the turn this conversation had taken. He was starting to become uncomfortable.

Hans picked up a pen off Erik's desk. "Give me that document you wanted me to sign," he said, resolutely.

Erik looked at Hans silently for about ten seconds. "Are you sure, Hans? This is a dangerous…"

"Give it to me," Hans said, louder and cutting in.

MAUTHAUSEN, AUSTRIA

It was an overcast and gray afternoon when Marina found herself tying a tourniquet to the arm of a twelve year old boy who had somehow gashed himself working in the camp. These were her children now, and she was determined to be with them until the end. Marina had chronic breathing problems, as well as stomach pain, which had worsened over the past year. She was getting weaker. She knew, deep down, that if something didn't change soon, she would meet her end.

When the tourniquet was tied, she told the boy it would heal him. Silently, she worried there might be an infection of some sort. The boy leaned against one of the crude wooden buildings of the camp while Marina caressed his hair. She found herself looking at a sequence of numbers engraved on the inside of the emaciated boy's other arm.

Then, out of the corner of her eye, she noticed a number of prisoners running toward the barb- wired fences separating the camp from the outside world. She turned her head towards the road and saw what seemed like an endless row of white ambulatory buses pulling up to the camp, just like the rumors had said. Marina felt her heart leap into her throat. Although it could've been another trick, another cruel lie, something told her it wasn't. To Marina, the white buses and their drivers did indeed look like angels, magically appearing out of thin air.

Hans was driving the lead bus. It was the most dangerous position, as a land mine would have killed him, and warned the others. For this reason, the nurses and other medical personnel rode on the other buses, and Hans had thus made the journey alone. He pulled up far enough so that all the other buses could get close to the main gate. Then, he got out and started walking towards the gate.

One of the few remaining Nazi guards at Mauthausen opened the main gate and walked away. Hans saw one of the nurses, the one who was known to speak both Polish and Swedish, having a somewhat contentious discussion with a young woman prisoner. The woman had five or six children huddled behind near her legs. Some prisoners were rushing onto the buses, but this woman seemed to be taking a cautious approach to the situation. The nurse turned to Hans. "She wants to talk to the head driver, not to me. I will have to translate. She says those children behind her aren't going anywhere unless she gets some answers she wants. I'm not sure she trusts us."

Hans looked at the woman. She was pale and emaciated and she was limping towards him. She looked at Hans and said something in Polish.

"She says her name is Marina and she has some questions before these children, or herself, get on the buses," the nurse advised.

"Tell her I'm Hans, and I'm the person she wants to talk to," the driver replied.

Hans noticed the woman looking at his chest and neck area. She appeared to be looking at his necklace, which held a crucifix.

"Where are you taking us?"

Hans listened to the nurse's translation and responded, "You're going to Sweden. There, doctors will administer medical…" Hans stopped in mid-sentence. He found himself looking at the prisoners, hundreds of them, waiting to get on the buses. He was stunned by their physical condition. They were emaciated, pale, and seemingly at death's door, just like Marina.

The nurse translated, presumably finishing the sentence Hans had been unable to. Marina could see the shock on Hans' face, and on the nurse's as well, for that matter.

"I suppose you're wondering what happened here," she offered. "Well, you see, Christians did this to us." She seemed to be looking through Hans, rather than at him, when she spoke.

Upon hearing the translation, Hans looked around at the prisoners again. After a short while, he responded, "Whoever did this to you were not Christians." He waited for the translation and for Marina's response. She said nothing.

"The long term plan is for the refugees, uh, the people at this camp to become either Swedish or Norwegian citizens. Our goal is for all of you to be healthy, productive members of our countries," Hans advised. It was clear to Hans that Marina did not trust him. Not yet, at least.

"Will we have to go through Nazi checkpoints?" she asked.

"No, the Nazis are in retreat now. The allies are crushing them. No checkpoints," Hans replied, searching her face for signs her skepticism may be relenting. Marina's face gave nothing away.

"What about you? Why did you, personally, agree to do this task?" she inquired. Her tone was as detached as it could be when asking a personal question.

Upon hearing the nurses' translation, Hans paused for some time. He found himself looking at the emaciated children as they waited in line to get on the buses. Then, he turned his attention back to Marina. "I have a six year old boy at home," he began. "A parent to one child is a parent to all children."

Upon hearing the translation of that statement, Marina was silent and motionless for some time. Hans fixed his eyes on her. He was uncertain of where things now stood. Her response seemed to be taking a long time in coming, and Hans was beginning to get uneasy about how this encounter was unfolding.

Suddenly, Marina leaned forward into Hans' chest and wrapped her arms around his neck. She pulled him very close. Hans had not been embraced by a woman that way since his wife had passed away more than two years before.

STOCKHOLM

On October 16, 1966, Hans stood near the fleet of buses warming up for the morning run in Stockholm's Central Bus Terminal. After thirty years on the job, he was reflecting on his career and, to an extent, on his life. Today, he would be getting behind the wheel for the last time. Incredibly, he had never been in an accident, and was regarded as the safest driver in the transit authority's history. He thought about the people he'd worked with through the years. There had been some real characters. Some in a good way, and some in a bad way. He thought of some of the special assignments he'd been tapped for. In 1960, he had taken the Swedish Olympic Hockey Team to the airport for their flight to the Olympic Games. Foremost in his mind, however, were the Holocaust survivors he had delivered to safety in the spring of 1945. One of those survivors, a teenage boy at the time, had gone on to become an important doctor in Stockholm. Hans had vivid memories of the strong willed woman with a limp who had questioned him at the gate, safeguarding the children who had, by circumstance, become her responsibility. She was now a teacher in Uppsala. Her daughter, who had survived the Holocaust, joined her in Sweden in the fall of 1945.

Hans couldn't put his finger on it, exactly, but he had been changed by the experience. He viewed himself, and his profession, differently afterward. The ill-informed views of those who saw him as "only a bus driver" or who otherwise belittled the great skills it took to post a safety record like his were trivial and irrelevant after he returned from Austria. He had come to see his role in life (perhaps a small role, perhaps not), as part of something larger and more important. For the rest of his life, he had stepped up whenever responsibilities chose him. He had gotten remarried and had a daughter who was now in college and studying to become a nurse. His son, Peter, was now 27 and an airline pilot in Copenhagen. And as for his other passengers, the vast majority were merely trying to get from point A to point B as part of a routine errand or part of their daily lives. Over the course of thirty years and more than a million passengers, however, Hans realized that not all of them were. Who could say that no one had ever run from an abusive situation at home, hopped on his bus, and never looked back? Who could say how many people had taken his bus to a better life?

"Last run today, Hans? How do you feel?" Ian, a mechanic for the transit authority, appeared with coffee in his hands. "Here, this is for you," he continued.

"Thanks," Hans replied.

The two old friends stood in the "yard," as it was known, looking at the big buses as they emitted diesel exhaust into the cold, dark morning. "You know, some people say these buses are ugly, but I never thought so," Ian offered.

Hans continued gazing at the buses for a few seconds before responding. "Come to think of it, Ian, I never thought so either."

Early Morning
In Baton Rouge

Mark came upon the road block and detour at around 11:45 p. m. This was quite unfortunate, as he wasn't expecting it and didn't know the area especially well. Despite the hour, a traffic jam was forming and the cars were being re-routed. Mark decided to forego the prescribed detour route and turned his motorcycle down a side street named Elmwood Avenue. The street was not well lit, but he drove it a fair distance before taking a left onto another side street named Auckland Road. He was hoping it would lead to another left and back onto the main road, past the road block.

Auckland Road was even darker than Elmwood Avenue. Mark passed some run down looking houses and trailers before coming to a dead end. Disappointed, he circled around and started heading back towards Elmwood. He really didn't want to get stuck in the traffic on the detour route, but didn't want to be lost in this part of Baton Rouge at this late hour, either. At the corner of Auckland and Elmwood, he stopped and let the motorcycle idle under one of the area's few streetlights. He then took out a city map and started searching for an alternative.

He liked Baton Rouge, but had never been in love with it, nor with Louisiana in general. It was late August and, being from Maine, he wasn't used to this kind of heat or humidity. Even at night, it seemed oppressive to him. The project he'd come here to work on was finally done (it had taken more than eight months to do) and he would be leaving for home in a few days. He was looking forward to it.

Mark was having trouble even finding Elmwood Avenue on the map, let alone tracing out an escape route by it. Suddenly, to his right, he heard some sort of commotion developing from a decrepit house on the corner of Auckland and Elmwood. He looked over his right shoulder and saw a woman, perhaps in her early twenties, running in his direction at full speed. She was wearing only her underwear. She was thin and appeared to have rather long legs as she ran barefoot towards the motorcycle, in great distress. As she closed in on him, Mark considered revving up the bike and taking off. However, something in him hesitated to do so.

"Get out of here!" the woman yelled as she hopped deftly onto the back of the motorcycle, wrapping her arms tightly around Mark's mid- section. Mark did rev up the engine and quickly took a left onto Elmwood, away from the main road, hoping blindly it would lead somewhere familiar. He traveled on the double line in the middle of the road to get around the traffic, something he would not have done under normal circumstances. He drove several miles as the half- naked stranger clung to him. He took a left, then a right, and then into a church parking lot.

"Why did you stop? Go behind the church building and stop there, don't stop out here," she said, looking around her. Mark complied. He stopped the bike behind the church, shut off the engine and put the keys in his pocket. Then he took off his helmet and turned to look over his shoulder at the passenger. "What's this all about?" he demanded.

"You need to help me…" she began. "I am in trouble. My boyfriend caught me in bed with another guy just before you pulled up. I have seen him angry and wild eyed before, especially when he's drinking hard, but never like that. I honestly believed he was about to kill me."

Mark looked into her face and could see she was genuinely terrified. If she was acting or feeding him a tale, she was doing a damn good job of it. Indeed, her account seemed quite plausible to him, given the totality of the circumstances. Mark was about to ask more questions, but again hesitated for a few moments. He found himself gazing into her face with a sense of curiosity. She was not a classic beauty, nor was ugly, but there was a unique quirkiness to her face which he couldn't put his finger on. Something was slightly "off" about her features, but in a good way. Whatever it was, it held his curiosity and he couldn't seem to turn from it. Maybe that was why he didn't just take off on the bike and leave her standing there. He would later claim, of course, that no self- respecting man would abandon a damsel in distress, etc., but it was really her mystique which had held his attention just long enough to enable her to reach the bike and get away.

"Well, where do you live? Where should I take you?"

"At that house, the house I ran from, that's where I live. You can't take me there. I live there with my boyfriend. You can't take me there. He is going to kill me. In fact, he may have already killed Walt…"

"Walt? Whose Walt?" Mark interrupted as he tried to sort this all out in his head.

"Walt is the guy I was making it with when…"

"Oh, right," Mark interrupted again. "Okay, go ahead, what were you saying?"

She took a couple of deep breaths and wiped a tear from her right eye with her right index finger. "He smashed Walt. I mean really leveled him. He landed eight or nine punches to Walt's face, four or five after he was down. I tried to stop him and that's when he turned towards me. Like I said, I had never seen him looking quite like that. He cocked his arm back and took a swing with all his might, stepping into the punch, but I ducked him and started running."

The she broke down sobbing, burying her face in her hands. Mark stepped off of the motorcycle. He wasn't sure what to do at this point. He figured there must be somewhere she could go, a relative's house or a battered women's shelter or something. He walked behind the motorcycle, running his fingers over his goatee repeatedly. He turned in her direction to speak, but then paused for a moment. Her face was still in her hands, and her head was shaking back and forth. She knew her life was a mess.

He looked her up and down from the side. She was slender and long legged. Her long, dark brown hair flowed about half way down the pale white skin of her back.

Mark took a deep breath and regained his composure. He walked around to the front of the motorcycle, putting his hands on the handlebars as he faced her, the wheel between his legs. She looked up at him, still upset but attempting to get a hold of herself.

"How did I end up like this?" she wondered aloud. His guess, it seemed, would be as good as hers.

"You need to stay the night somewhere. Then you can figure the rest of it out in the morning. I'll take you to your parent's or sister's or something…"

"I don't have parents," she stated abruptly.

Mark was taken aback. His face reflected his bewilderment as he raised one eye brow at her.

"I mean, I have them, but I ran away from them three years ago, when I was sixteen. I ran away with Steve…"

"Whose Steve?" Mark wondered, interrupting again.

"Steve is my boyfriend. He is the guy who just tried to…"

"Oh, I see. So you've been with this guy for a while," Mark observed, interrupting once again. "How old is Steve?"

"He's twenty eight. No, wait, twenty nine. His birthday was a couple of weeks ago…"

"So you're nineteen and he's twenty nine now? He is ten years older than you? Is that right? Is my math correct?"

She looked at him and nodded slowly. It seemed like a question she didn't want to answer.

"So he was twenty six and you were sixteen when he took you away from…"

"Yes," she stated curtly. She would not have been answering these questions under most circumstances. It was not something she was comfortable talking about.

"Well you must have other relatives, like an aunt or something…"

"I ran from Oklahoma. That's where all my relatives are, except one uncle who lives in California, last I knew." She was getting very anxious. She didn't want Mark to part with her. She needed to be with him, at least for the night. There was something about him she was clinging to. She had felt it on the motorcycle as she wrapped her near nude body around him, her life possibly hanging in the balance. He had driven away decisively, without hesitation, and he could handle the motorcycle well at high speeds and around corners. She sensed that he was a responsible person of action, a do-er instead of a talker.

"Please, just for tonight, take me to your place. I promise I will leave in the morning. Steve knows all the battered women's shelters around here, I've been in them before. When I was under eighteen, I used a fake name and date of birth when I checked into them. He will find me there," she continued.

Mark was a pretty good judge of other's emotions. The desperation in her voice seemed real to him. Mark began weighing his options. There was a dead bolt lock on his bedroom door. (The prior tenant had had it installed after an intruder had broken in late at night). Even still, he knew that taking her in, even for one night, posed a risk. She herself could be dangerous, although he was slowly forming the impression she probably wasn't. He took a good look at her pleading face. In the corner of his right eye, he noticed a large wooden cross on the side lawn of the church. Then he walked around to the side of the motorcycle.

"Okay, one night, but that's it. You must leave tomorrow morning without question. Do you understand?"

She breathed a big sigh of relief, then replied, "Yes, yes, I'll leave in the morning. Thank you so much…" She leaned to her left, still seated on the bike, and hugged him as best she could without getting off the bike.

"What's your name, anyway?" he asked her. His tone acknowledged the irony in that they still didn't know each other's names even though, at that point, they had been involved in what seemed like a significant moment in each other's life.

"Ashley," she replied, catching her breath as her emotion shifted from fear and anxiety to relief and, at least for the moment, joy. "I'm Ashley," she repeated, looking at him and smiling broadly. He gazed back at her, and again did so for just a second or two longer than what was typical for him. At that moment, her face was beaming and her eyes appeared to glisten, even though this night was moonless and pitch black.

"I'm Mark," he responded as he hopped on the bike and positioned himself in front of her. Mark was six foot one and thin. He was twenty five years old and owned a commercial construction company he had inherited from his dad. He started learning the ropes about ten years prior, when he was still in high school. He was reluctant, at first, to take the contract to build a large supermarket in Baton Rouge, but the money was too good to pass up. The supermarket chain accepted his first bid, without even negotiating first. Leaving home for a while was doable for him because he was single and didn't have a girlfriend (he'd recently broken up with someone back in Maine). He was glad the project was finally finishing up. It had been a hot, humid and difficult summer.

The Harley Davidson pulled up to the apartment building. Mark's leased one bedroom was on the third floor. He hoped it was so late that no one would notice the almost nude lady accompanying him to his apartment.

"You can take a shower if you want, then we'll get you into some clothes even though I'm sure they'll be too big," he offered as they entered the apartment. "There's a pullout couch and I'll get it ready for you while you're in the shower."

"Thanks so much, I can't tell you how much this means. I'm so glad you're helping me out," she replied. Her gratitude was genuine.

It was 1:15 a. m. when Ashley appeared from the bathroom in mark's oversized T-shirt and boxer shorts, her hair still wet as she tried to dry it with a blue towel. She had taken a long shower, it seemed to Mark. He watched as she turned her head to the side, allowing her long hair to hang down so she could work on it with the towel. It was a nice apartment, with central air conditioning, and he noticed she was starting to shiver. He retrieved a bath robe from the closet, a well made garment he had bought in Maine. She thanked him before wrapping the robe around her, almost as if it was were a blanket. She looked to her right and saw that the couch was pulled out and ready for her to sleep on.

"I'm having some iced tea, would you like some?" he offered, watching her carefully. He wasn't sure how tired she was. He felt a need to unwind before going to bed. He had been restless all night, which is why he'd gone cruising in the first place. He had taken off on a whim at about ten o'clock that night.

"Sure," she replied. They sat in the kitchen, around the circular dinner table under a globe light. Her back was to the refrigerator and she had a good view of much of the apartment. "Nice place you have here," she offered. It was certainly nicer than anywhere she'd ever lived. "Where are you from? You have a fierce northern accent," she said, smiling.

"I'm from Maine," he replied, "Have you ever been there?"

"No, I sure haven't, what's it like?" she was still smiling.

"Hmmm…what's it like, how could I describe it? Well, when you first cross the border from New Hampshire, you know what the welcome sign says, besides 'Welcome to Maine'?"

"No, what does it say?" Her smile was fading but still there. She had a far away, whimsical look on her face.

"It says, 'Welcome to Maine, The Way Life Should Be'," he advised.

Her smile disappeared completely and her face adopted a serious and interested posture. "That's what it says? 'The way life should be'? It says that?"

"Yeah, that's what it says on the sign," he reiterated. He was watching her closely. Her face was giving something away, but he wasn't sure what. She wasn't a poker player, he concluded. "In some ways it's true about Maine, and in some ways it's not. There aren't a whole lot of people, or cars, or pollution there. There's very little crime. It's quite beautiful there, also. But a lot of people wouldn't want to be there in January or February. Life isn't how it should be then," he stated, smirking a little.

"Why not?" she wondered. Mark reasoned she'd never been to the north in the winter time.

"Because it's zero degrees in the middle of the daytime, not even counting the wind chill," he replied with a chuckle.

"Oh, that's really cold," she opined in response. Something told Mark she wasn't as cutely naïve as she seemed at the moment. People are different at 1:45 a. m. than they are during business hours, he reckoned as he glanced at the clock on the wall.

He suddenly realized that his right hand had been taken into custody by her hands. Her right palm rested beneath his while her left claimed his hand's top side.

"I want you to know, in seriousness, how thankful I am for what you have done for me tonight. It is quite possible you saved my life," she reminded him. He kept his hand between hers and did not move it. His face now became serious.

"Look," he began cautiously, his eyes now piercing into her. "I know you were uncomfortable earlier when I asked you about your history. When we were talking about how you ran from Oklahoma when you were sixteen and Steve, or whatever his name is, was twenty six. I know you were with this guy Walt because your boyfriend isn't the answer for you. Your boyfriend is one of those people who doesn't get it, isn't he?"

Ashley let go of his hand and folded her arms, looking away for a moment. She noticed a small wooden cross hanging on the wall. "What do you mean?" she asked, as her eyes returned to his.

Mark took a swill of his iced tea. "I think you know what I mean, he's just not…he doesn't get it," he continued.

She appeared confused. She tightened the belt of the bath robe around her waist.

Mark was perplexed by her lack of insight. It was as if she thought of Steve as a typical or normal guy. He let go of his glass and brought his hands together, clasping the fingers of his right hand over the fingers of his left and vice versa. His elbows were on the table and his hands formed a support base for his chin. There was a long pause.

Mark then said, in a soft tone, "Someone hurt you very bad once, didn't they?"

She looked up at him, her arms still folded. "I told you, Steve has beat me up a bunch of..."

"Before that," Mark interrupted. "I mean before that, before Steve."

Ashley's face suddenly flushed red. Her throat visibly swallowed a lump and her chest inflated and deflated with heavier breaths. Slowly, she began nodding her head at him, unable to answer verbally. She brought her elbows to the table and buried her face in her hands as she began to sob.

Mark rose from his chair and stood beside her, looking down at her. "I'm very, very sorry," he said with empathy, placing his hand on her shoulder. She wiped away the tears as best she could, still heaving deep breaths. Slowly, she pushed herself up from the chair and turned toward him. She wrapped her arms around his neck and pulled him closer, hoping for a moment that he would never let go of her.

The embrace lasted for some time as she sobbed quietly into his chest. Finally, she looked up at him as her arms continued clutching around his neck. "I often have nightmares," she revealed, catching her breath. "Bad ones. Terrifying nightmares. I don't know if it's because of the things that have happened to me in my life or what. I don't want to sleep alone tonight after what happened earlier. Please stay with me. I'll behave, I promise. I just don't want to be alone on that pullout couch." He looked down at her, enfolding her in his arms as he silently nodded to her in assent.

Ashley was exhausted when she curled up next to her host's body at 2:20 a. m. He wore a T shirt and cotton shorts and pretended to be more tired than he was. She fell asleep very quickly as her head rested on his chest. They were covered by a red and black checkered blanket he had brought from

Maine. He would remain awake for another hour, thinking a great deal about the eventful night he'd had and the mysterious young woman in his arms.

At one point, her hands fastened onto his left bicep and wouldn't let go. She was asleep when this happened, it was an unconscious act on her part. He looked over at her and gazed at her as she slept. He didn't mind that she had claimed his arm, perhaps it was staving off the nightmares she had feared. On two occasions, her grip on his bicep loosened slowly and almost leg go as she slept. At the last moment, however, she would retake the muscle back into her hands with some urgency, as if subconsciously realizing it had almost slipped from her grasp. He deliberately remained still, allowing her continued access to his arm as it seemed to adopt a life-raft type quality for her.

At around 3:30, he finally fell asleep. Soon, he was having a strange dream about a large and empty cargo ship drifting aimlessly in a thick, foggy ocean. It didn't seem to Mark like anyone was on or directing the ship. He couldn't seem to figure out where it had come from or where it was going to. It just continued its aimless drift as the fog got thicker and grayer.

A ray of sunlight crossed Mark's face shortly after six a. m., awakening him into a groggy state. Suddenly, he remembered there was a woman – a stranger, for all intents and purposes- lying next to him and looking up at him. Her head was on his chest and her arms were around his mid- section. "Good morning," she offered softly as she smiled at him. Turning her head down, she began talking to his chest instead of to his face. "Why does it feel better in your arms?"

Mark had heard that question twice before, as two women from his past had wondered the very same thing. He never answered the question verbally, he just pulled the woman closer. Ashley smiled as he did so.

There are two types of men: givers and takers. When a man is a giver, it comes through in the way he holds a woman. Women eventually value that more than whatever they get out of the takers. Ashley was learning this for the first time as she lay with Mark.

They both went back to sleep. She woke up again around 8:30 a. m. and took another shower. A half an hour later, she came out of the bathroom in Mark's bath robe, her hair wet again. She was surprised to find he had awakened and was sipping coffee as he gazed at her from the chair he was reclining in.

Mark had opened the shades and light filled the room through the windows. She was attempting to dry her hair again with the towel when, suddenly, she stopped. Looking at him, she asked, "What?...What is it?"

Mark stood up from the recliner. "You're beautiful," he stated with conviction in his northern accent.

A smile from ear to ear erupted on her face. "You...you think so?" she managed, seemingly holding back tears of surprised joy.

"Yes, I do," he replied, definitively. "You are a knockout."

Ashley's chest inflated and deflated with deep breaths again. She was speechless, but her face said it all. She was overjoyed.

Mark walked over to her and kissed her passionately on the lips. He took her body into his arms securely. Their foreheads met gently at the conclusion of the kiss, as she looked directly into his eyes.

"Take me to where you're from. Take me to the place where life is like it should be. I don't care if it goes to thirty below zero."

"I will," he replied without hesitation. "I will take you there. You are coming with me," he said. Then he resumed kissing her passionately.

It was 9:15 a.m.

"We May be on Our Own"

Sara, aged four, was not happy about having to go to the corner market with her mother on a December morning in 1917. It was too cold for the five block stroll, she felt. Further, her friend and next door neighbor, Julie, might not want to play later. She wanted to get to Julie's house to play as soon as possible.

"We've run out of a few things," her mother, Jacqueline, offered in explanation. The errand was, she assured her daughter, quite necessary. Sara, however, continued to believe the errand was "stupid," but only dared to vocalize her view once. Her mother had quickly admonished her to watch her language when she did.

"Good day, Miss, is your husband still out at sea?" The store's owner inquired of Jacqueline as she approached the counter. His name was Archie White. He was a heavy-set man in his mid-forties, and he knew just about everyone in the Richmond neighborhood of Halifax's North End. He also seemed to know everyone's business, as most people in the neighborhood would pause for a conversation during their frequent visits. Some even picked up their mail at the store.

"Yes, the *Maria Jane* won't be back for another week. They're trolling the Grand Banks, off Newfoundland. It's a long trip, but I'm just glad he's not in the Bay of Fundy. Too many ships don't come back from there."

"I guess you're right, Miss, quite a few of them…"

The next thing Sara heard was an incredibly loud explosion. Her mother grabbed her and ran with her to a back corner of the store. Her mother tried to tell her something as they crouched down on the floor, but a second (even louder) explosion drowned out whatever her mother had to say.

"How bad is it? Do we know?" Rebecca Sweet asked Agnes, one of the other nurses on the train, as it raced through Maine on its way to Canada.

"No one knows, the reports were sketchy. It's not good, let's put it that way," Agnes replied. Agnes was older than Rebecca and had seen more in her long nursing career. This wasn't the first disaster she'd dealt with.

"I wonder how much longer it will be until we get there?" Rebecca pondered aloud. She seemed to be seeking leadership, as opposed to information, from the more experienced nurse.

"We should be there by late tonight. Maybe early tomorrow."

Sara asked her mother about Julie, to which Jacqueline replied, "I'm sure Julie is fine." In fact, Jacqueline had no idea if Julie was even alive, let alone "fine." She wasn't sure if her four-year old daughter had bought into her reassurance or not. She considered it possible that Sara would call her bluff, so she quickly changed the subject. They had spent the night in a makeshift shelter for women and children. It was cold with no running water. The men had taken up in an abandoned, boarded up house which was still standing after the explosions had ended. Archie White was not among them. He'd died after being struck in the head by an airborne board within seconds of the first explosion.

The mother and daughter were now walking amongst the wreckage, looking for people they knew. They were still unaware of the fate of numerous acquaintances and neighbors. It was December 7th, and snow was falling heavily on the smoldering remains of more than 1700 buildings.

"Why did it happen, mom? When will dad be back?"

"We don't know why it happened, honey, but Dad will be back soon. He was out at sea when it happened, thank the Lord," Jacqueline replied, looking around in all directions. "I've never seen anything like this, Sara," she continued, shaking her head. "Never."

"Why are we stopped?" Rebecca wondered. Neither she nor Agnes had slept much.

"Somebody said something about the snow blocking the rails, so the men are out there shoveling," Agnes advised her.

Rebecca looked at her watch. It was just past midnight.

"Does anyone know? Anyone at all, in the outside world? Are the telegraphs working?" Jim Drayson, a long time Councillor for the North End, was sitting across from the Mayor of Halifax in City Hall. "And do we know how the hell this happened yet?"

The Mayor, Tristan Blake, took a deep breath. "Apparently, a boat carrying lots of explosives collided with another boat in the harbor. My guess is the explosives were headed for Europe, to help in the war effort. Good thing this will be the last war. But to answer your first question, the telegraph lines were severed in the explosion. We have not been able to communicate. I simply do not know if anyone outside the province knows what's going on, and I'm certain they don't know the extent of it."

Mayor Blake, usually an energetic type, was shaken and slowed by what had happened. He leaned forward and folded his hands on the desk as he looked at the Councillor. "I simply don't know if we'll get help from the outside or not. We may be on our own," he acknowledged. This observation was followed by a silent pause, as the two men just looked at each other for a short time.

"Well, do we know how many people didn't make it? How many people died?"

Mayor Blake's hands came together as a kind of two handed fist, against which his forehead rested. After a moment, he put his hands down on the desk, and looked into his old friend's eyes. Blake's head then shook back and forth, silently.

Jim Drayson couldn't sleep that night. He left a note for his wife and walked out to the street. Although it seemed hopeless, he started cleaning debris from the streets with his bare hands. Maybe he could salvage something, or someone. It seemed the sixty two- year old had more energy in him than he had realized.

"Why are you still out here, Jim? Go home, get some sleep. We'll get more done tomorrow that way," Wesley Aines, another longtime resident, had come upon Jim while cleaning debris from the street himself at around 2:45 a.m.

"I couldn't sleep. How about you, Wesley, what are you doing out here?"

"Same thing, couldn't sleep. What did the Mayor say?"

"Not much. I don't think he knows much. I saw him around eight o'clock tonight. He was practically falling asleep right there at his desk. He had a long, long day."

The two men spent the next ten minutes cleaning debris and comparing notes as to which of their mutual acquaintances were still alive, and which were not.

"You know that Archie passed away, right? Archie White. He was inside his store, where he always was…" Jim began, only to be loudly interrupted.

"Listen!" Wesley yelled, as he leaned forward with his hands on his knees, as though leaning forward would improve his ability to hear.

Jim Drayson and Wesley Aines arrived at the train station, on foot and out of breath, just after 3:00 a.m. They ran six blocks, not a small feat for a couple of older men at that time of night. But their curiosity got the better of them. Who was on the train? Where had they come from? Ottawa? Montreal? Even America? Did they know the extent of the disaster, and how much could they help?

As soon as the train came to a stop, people started filing out. They each held some sort of medical bag or equipment, and they were led by a tall and thin man in his fifties. Jim Drayson approached the man. "Good evening, sir, I am an Councillor in the city. I take it you have some understanding of what has happened here?"

"We do indeed," replied the visitor. "I'm Dr. Bernard Morley. We are here on the orders of the Governor of Massachusetts, in the United States. There are more on the way. More trains, medics, construction workers and supplies.

This is only the beginning. Take us to where the injured people are."

Rebecca treated the injured's wounds from about 3:30 to 7:30 a. m. that morning. The twenty four year old nurse then succumbed to fatigue and slept for about two hours on the bare floor of the makeshift clinic inside City Hall. Upon waking, she realized that a young girl was standing above her, looking down at her. Rebecca rose to a sitting position as she wiped the sleep from her eyes. "Why, hello," she offered to the young girl. The girl was awfully cute, Rebecca noted. "What's your name?"

"My name is Sara."

The girl seemed quite shy to Rebecca. It was as if she had something to say, but couldn't put the words together in her head. Finally, she did speak up. "When I grow up, I want to be a nurse like you. And I want to look like you, too."

Rebecca was touched by the sweet and pleasant child. "Nursing is a very rewarding profession," she concurred.

"Where did you come from?" Sara inquired, her eyes widening.

"Well, we came from Boston. It's a long, long way from here. We took a train to get here."

"You came that far just to help us?"

"Well, of course we did. It's Christmas time, after all."

Sara folded her arms. She had forgotten it was the Christmas Season. "Do you think Santa Claus will still come here this year?"

Rebecca chuckled. "Yes, I'm sure Santa Claus will still come here this year. He might not bring as many presents as he brought last year, but he will come."

Rebecca gave the toddler a big hug before turning her attention back to the injured.

Sara was not as optimistic about Santa Claus as Rebecca was. She had seen all the destroyed houses, including her own. There were no chimneys for Santa to go down. There were no Christmas trees under which he could put the presents. And where would the parents keep the presents, anyway? Most of them didn't even have houses. As she contemplated these questions, standing in the foyer of City Hall, she felt as if she were about to cry. Just then, however, she could see from the corner of her right eye that something was coming towards her very quickly. Alarmed, she turned to her right and realized a young girl was running towards her. Upon realizing it was Julie, Sara's arms opened widely as her friend ran into her, engulfing her in as big a bear hug as a four year old could muster. It was one of the happiest moments of Sara's young life.

Dr. Morley had his hands full, and he was tired. One patient after another, and then another. Some could be helped, some couldn't. After wrapping a young boy's arm in a splint, it occurred to the doctor that he was being followed. He turned around to find Jim Drayson following him.

"What is it, Councillor? How can I help you?"

"I just wanted to tell you, Doctor, the people of this city will never forget what you and your friends from Boston are doing for us."

"Thank you, Sir, that's very kind of you to say."

The doctor then turned his attention to another patient. She was an older woman who needed the dressing changed on a wound. He removed the old dressing, cleaned the wound, and then applied new dressing and gauze. The woman thanked him, and he turned around to search for another patient to treat. As he did so, he bumped into Jim Drayson again, this time constituting somewhat of a collision.

"Look, Councillor, I need more space to…"

"Never," the old statesman repeated, driving home the point he'd made earlier.

ONE HUNDRED YEARS LATER

In December, 2017, four year old Elizabeth Witton stood on the grounds of the Massachusetts State Capitol in Boston, admiring the very tall and beautifully lit Christmas tree on the State House lawn.

"Mommy, that's a really big tree," the toddler observed. Her mother Carol, a state legislator, was also focused on the tree. "It certainly is," she concurred.

"I've never seen a tree that big, mom. Where did it come from?"

"Actually, honey, every year Boston's official tree is a gift from Nova Scotia."

"Who?"

"It's a place in Canada. It's a long, long way from here."

The girl held her mother's hand. She briefly wondered if there were reindeers in Canada.

"Mom, why do they send us a big Christmas tree every year?"

The legislator was familiar with the tradition. "A long time ago, Massachusetts helped them when the really needed help. They never forgot the help we gave them, so every year they send us a big tree for Christmas."

A breeze came through and Elizabeth hugged her mother's leg for warmth.

"How long ago did this happen, mom? That we helped them out?"

Carol reached down and touched her daughter's head as she continued to gaze at the hundreds of lights adorning the tree.

"Well I guess it's been about a hundred years or so, now that you bring it up."

"Oh, wow. That's a very long time. They must have very good memories, those people who sent us the tree."

Carol smiled and looked down at her daughter. "Yes, honey. I suppose they do."

To this day, the Commonwealth of Massachusetts is annually gifted its large, official Christmas Tree from the Province of Nova Scotia in remembrance and gratitude for its assistance more than one hundred years ago.

White Mountains

I. STATE POLICE HEADQUARTERS, CONCORD, NEW HAMPSHIRE, JUNE 22, 2014

"You look tired, Chief," State Police Detective Rick Earls noted, sizing up his superior.

"I didn't sleep much. My wife's anxieties are starting to act up again," Chief Hogan replied.

"Oh, I'm sorry to hear that boss," offered the detective. Their discussion was taking place in the detective's office, a departure from usual, since the chief usually summoned Rick to his office whenever a meeting was necessary. This meeting, however, would not be typical or ordinary, as Rick well knew. The chief came straight to his office as soon as he walked in the door this morning, and Rick knew why.

"So give me an update on the McConnell case," implored the chief, hoping against reason some new information had emerged overnight.

"Sorry, Chief, nothing new," answered the detective. It was an uncomfortable situation for both of them.

"As you know, Rick, the media is pushing us for updates on this one. The public – and the family- want the information as soon as possible. Even the governor called me about it last night. People are just very intrigued by her disappearance."

"I get that, Chief. We are devoting all available resources to this one. I temporarily reassigned Jack Holloway to this, off the identity theft investigation he was doing. There just aren't any new leads since we last spoke."

"Man, we don't have much, do we?" observed the chief. "Alright, tell me again what we do know. Take it from the top."

Detective Earls took a sip of the decaffeinated coffee he kept in a thermos on his desk. Caffeine bothered his stomach.

"All right, Chief. Mrs. McConnell woke up on the morning of June 14, a Sunday, at the hotel over on Penrod Road and found her husband unresponsive. He was lying in bed next to her and she knew something was seriously wrong. She dialed 911 from the hotel phone next to the bed. An ambulance came and took them both to Central Hospital. He was declared dead on arrival by the ER doctor, Dr. Morris."

"Okay, I'm with you so far, then what," urged the chief as he adjusted himself in his chair. In addition to a neurotic wife, he'd been having back pain lately.

"Well, then a social worker, Mr. Dave Hammond, was assigned to grief counsel and otherwise assist Mrs. McConnell until a family member or someone arrived. So he took her aside, into a private room. He started in with the usual condolences and grief talk, then about the logistics. You know, where is the nearest family member, how can they be contacted and so on. He didn't think she was fit to be alone at the time."

Rick paused and took another sip of his decaf.

"So according to Dave, he continued doing the social worker thing, telling her about local funeral services, grief counseling, the hospital chaplain…"

"Where were these people from again?" the chief interrupted.

"Connecticut, near Mystic, about three and a half hours away. They were visiting a daughter here in Concord, because it was one of the grandkids' birthday, or something. Anyway, Dave said Mrs. McConnell went into a sort of daze at that point. Like she was somewhere else entirely, in a trance. Dave's words were going in one ear and out the other, it seemed. After all, these people had been married for forty three years. Dave decided he had better leave her alone for a couple of minutes, to collect herself. So he stepped out of the room and sat nearby."

"Well, didn't he notice her leaving, then?"

"Apparently, she came out of the room and said she had to go to the ladies' room. Dave directed her to it and then watched her walk down the hall until she entered the women's room. She did go in, he said. After a little while he started reviewing his notes. A while after that, he looked up and noticed Mrs. McConnell had not returned from the ladies' room yet. He asked the receptionist to go check on her, which she did. Then the receptionist came back and said there was no sign of her in there. All the employees were put on alert in case they saw her wandering the halls. The Concord police were notified. But there just wasn't any sign of her. The next day, Concord referred the case to us. They didn't want to touch it."

"Well, let me ask you this, Rick," the chief implored, trying to hide his disappointment in the slowness of the investigation. "Is there any doubt in your mind that Mr. McConnell died of natural causes?"

Rick ran his hand over his beard as he looked at the chief. "Chief, there is no doubt in my mind. The coroner ruled definitively it was a cardiac arrest of natural origin. There was no poison or anything toxic in his system. He was sixty four years old with high blood pressure and high cholesterol."

II. CONCORD, NEW HAMPSHIRE, JUNE 24, 20014

Julie lay down next to her husband, Paul, after putting their two young children to bed. The light was still on as Paul had been reading. When Julie joined him, however, he put the book down and devoted his full attention to her. There had been times over the last few days when she seemed on the verge of breaking down. He was trying to be as attentive as possible, as her emotional state was a minute by minute issue.

"Mom became disoriented when they told her dad was gone. She became dislodged from reality. I know that's what happened. I think she is wandering the streets around here like a homeless person, like a bag lady, not even knowing who she is," she opined, seemingly to thin air rather than to Paul, as she was looking at the wall instead of him. Paul remained silent.

"Detective Earls said there's been no activity on her ATM card or credit cards or anything," she continued. "How is she surviving?" she wondered, quickly turning towards Paul.

She saw the look on his face the instant she asked her question. He tried to change it, but it was too late. She knew what he thought now: her mother was not surviving, her mother was dead.

"She wouldn't need money if she was eating at churches or a homeless shelter. She's pretty crafty and resourceful, I think she could make it on the streets," Paul opined, hoping his words would be a tourniquet, rather than a band aid, for Julie's emotional state.

The room went silent for about a minute. The she turned to her side, wrapping her arm around him and resting her head on his chest. "Paul, I feel guilty," she confessed.

"There was nothing you could have done. You got to the hospital as soon as you could have, and she was already gone."

"That's not what I mean," she retorted.

"What do you mean, then?" Paul asked, genuinely in the dark.

She let go of his chest, and went flat on her back next to him. "Growing up, other people's deaths were our currency, our business. People's deaths were stats on a piece of paper. The more deaths there were, the more money we made."

"Well, isn't that just the nature of the funeral business?" he replied.

"Yes, Paul, it is. But you're missing the point. When dad died and mom realized he was dead, well… I don't know. I'm sure the social worker brought up the subject of funeral arrangements. Maybe she felt guilty too, the way I do now. Maybe the guilt and grief combined were too much for her. Maybe that's why she broke with reality."

Again, Paul weighed in. "She had nothing to feel guilty about. That's just our system, that's capitalism…"

"I know what it is," she replied, cutting him off. Silence ensued for some time. "I'm sure you're right," Julie finally said, though her tone of voice suggested she was not convinced. "I'm sure I'm just reading into it too much."

III.   STATE POLICE HEADQUARTERS,
       CONCORD, NEW HAMPSHIRE, JUNE 27, 2014

Detective Earls scanned his e-mails, hoping for something on the McConnell case. It was 9:30 a. m. and the chief had already called him once. There was a knock on his door.

"Come in," he barked.

It was Officer Jack Hart. It had to be something important, as Jack would have phoned or e-mailed him if it had been routine. Rick invited him to sit down. Obliging, Jack folded his arms as he sat and looked at the detective.

"What is it?" Rick urged, a tinge of impatience in his voice.

"Well, there is someone here saying he has information on the McConnell case."

"Bring him in, then."

"Okay, Detective, but…"

"But what?"

"He's kind of…it seems to me… kind of 'slow.' There is something wrong with him. I'm not sure how credible or useful the information is going to be."

Rick took a deep breath at the prospect of another dead end. "Well, bring him in, let me see what he's got."

The young man was escorted into the detective's office by Officer Hart, who then left the room. Rick sized up the witness. He appeared to be in his mid-twenties. He was a little overweight and somewhat disheveled. His clothes didn't fit him right and didn't match. His haircut wouldn't be attracting attention from the ladies any time soon. Further, he couldn't seem to hold eye contact.

Rick stood up and shook the young man's hand. "Have a seat, I understand you have some information on the McConnell disappearance."

The young man sat down. "Yes sir, I mean, yes Detective. My name is Herb and I live here in Concord. I really look up to the police, like yourself. Once a police man helped me out when these guys were pushing me around."

"Glad we could help, son. What information do you have?"

"Well, firstly, what you need to know is, I have a photographic memory. Only, it's not really photographic because that means visual, but with me it is verbal. What I mean is, I remember each and every word I hear and the order the words were said in."

Rick raised his left eye brow. He wasn't sure what to make of the young man's claim. He thought it possible the claim was true, but wasn't totally buying it yet.

"Anyway," the witness continued, "I was over at the hotel, and I don't remember the name of it, but I was using their computer to check my e-mail and there was this other computer right next to me…"

"This was the hotel over on Penrod Road, I take it?" Rick interrupted.

"Yes, sir."

"Were you staying there?"

"Well, no sir, sorry sir. I mean, Detective. I just walked in and was using their computer."

The two looked at each other silently for a moment. Then Herb started looking around the room.

"All right, continue," Rick urged, trying to move things along.

"Well, this was around six p. m. on Saturday night, the 13th. That was the night before the lady disappeared, at least that's what the newspaper said."

The detective confirmed the witness' understanding, saying, "That's true, continue."

"You see, the McConnells came over and started using the computer right next to me, only I didn't know it was them at the time. I figured it out afterwards, when I read the newspaper and saw a picture of them and everything. Anyhow, Mrs. McConnell sat down at the computer and he stood behind her. She started typing some stuff in and then she said - and this is what I mean when I say I remember everything word for word – she said, 'I don't like what he did. I don't like the program. It's harder to use than the other one we had. There's too many icons and they're not self- explanatory.'"

Herb continued, "Then Mr. McConnell said, 'So far, I don't like it much either. Hey what's that one there? That one, on line forty two on the spread sheet? I don't remember that one.' Then she said, 'Oh, that was the young girl who was cremated, remember?'"

"Hold on, son," the detective interrupted. "Run that by me again, what Mrs. McConnell said."

Herb paused for a moment and looked at the detective. It was as if he had been replaying the scene in his mind on an audio tape playback and the detective had hit the pause button.

"Oh, yes, Detective. Mrs. McConnell was answering him what was on line forty two of the spread sheet and she said, 'Oh, that was the young girl who was cremated, remember?'"

Herb paused and looked at the detective. Rick was watching him closely. He wanted to see if Herb had a comment or observation of his own to make before continuing his statement. Instead Herb's eyes moved away from Rick's and up towards the plaques hanging on the wall behind him, which testified to the detective's distinguished career.

"Continue, son..."

"Well, then Mr. McConnell said, 'Oh, right, the girl who was cremated, I forgot about her. Then there's those other two, how come they're both on line forty three?' Then she said, 'See, that's what I mean. The lines on this spread sheet are too close together. The second one is on line forty four, you have to look really close.'"

The detective's face looked long and ashen, Herb noticed. He continued without interruption, however.

"Then he said, 'Oh, I see what you mean. You need a microscope to read this stupid thing. I take it those two were the couple in the car crash, right?' Then she said, 'Yes and the car caught on fire, too, so the embalmer had a tough time with them. He put in for an hour and a half overtime pay. He said he didn't get out until late that night.' Then, this is the only part I don't remember word for word, but I remember what she was talking about, though. She started complaining again about the program, something about how it makes you save your work twice instead of once…"

"Okay…Okay, Herb, what happened next?" urged the detective. His horrified curiosity was waning as his desire for something of investigative value was escalating.

Herb looked at Rick for about five seconds in silence. He was taken aback by the detective's seemingly lukewarm interest in his information.

"Well, then Mr. McConnell said, 'We've only got three this week. I thought there was more.' Then she said, 'Oh, well, that's only through Tuesday. There will probably be a couple more by the end of the week.' Then he said, 'Oh, that's right, by Friday there will probably be a couple more.' I remember he had a very annoying voice, Mr. McConnell did. He kept trying to clear his throat. Then he said to her, 'What if you hit control - alt – S to save…"

"Alright, Herb, alright," Rick said, interrupting the young man. This time he was hitting the stop button on Herb's play-back machine, rather than PAUSE. He took a deep breath and then had a sip from his ever present thermos. Leaning forward, he addressed the witness in a slightly sterner tone.

"Herb, listen. I want you to hold eye contact with me for a minute. Can you do that?"

Herb was nervous and perplexed. The interview had not gone as he expected. "Well, okay sir, I'll try, yes." He looked back at Rick, into his eyes.

"Are you certain, Herb, that both of them said that exact phrase. They both said, 'There will probably be a couple more by the end of the week'?"

"Yes, sir, I'm positive, sir," Herb replied with unwavering certainty. "Well, actually, Mr. McConnell said, 'There will probably be a couple more by Friday,' not, 'by the end of the week'…"

"I get it, Herb," replied Detective Earls, again interrupting as he sat back in his chair. "Well, thanks for coming in and giving us your information, Herb."

The witness looked at Rick in silence. "Well, Detective, does this help you understand how come Mrs. McConnell disappeared?"

"No, son, I'm afraid it doesn't."

The odd young man had a disappointed look on his face. "Well, that's too bad. I thought this was going to help you understand how come. Because, you know, they didn't care about the people who died."

Rick looked at the young man , then briefly down at the notes he had taken during the interview. "I don't see how this helps us, son. We already knew they owned a funeral home. I don't see how this is going to help us find her or know why she disappeared. Again, I want to thank you for coming in and trying to help. I do appreciate it."

Herb's mood seemed to brighten a little. He seemed to take pride in having fulfilled what he considered a civic duty. Smiling, he stood up and shook Detective Earls' hand. "Absolutely, my pleasure, Detective. They have my phone number out front, so call me if you need anything else, officer."

"Will do, Herb," promised the detective as the young man turned and walked away.

IV. RYE, NEW HAMPSHIRE,
     JUNE 30, 2014

Julie sat on the large rocks of Wallis Sands State Beach on New Hampshire's coast. She had dropped the kids off at day care even though she'd been taking time off and hadn't been going to work. She wanted to be alone at the beach, and had driven an hour and a half to get to this spot, which held memories from her childhood. The breeze off the ocean was cooler than usual for this time of year. She sat with her knees up and her arms wrapped around them. She spent a total of two hours there, shivering on occasion as she looked at the waves crash on the rocks, the wind blowing her long hair back.

V.   STATE POLICE HEADQUARTERS, CONCORD, NEW HAMPSHIRE, JULY 2, 2014

"Mrs. McConnell's body was found at the base of Cathedral Ledge by a hiker at around 8:45 this morning. Cathedral Ledge is in Hale's Location, an unincorporated area in the White Mountains, about sixty miles north of Concord. Her vehicle was found in the parking lot at the top of the mountain's access road, and had apparently been there since June 14th when she disappeared," Detective Earls announced, thus beginning the 6:00 p.m. press conference. "No one reported the car's presence at that location until we located it after the hiker's report today. We are looking into how the delay happened, but it appears people assumed the car belonged to hikers." The room was sparser than expected, with six reporters in attendance. Time had withered the public's interest in the case.

"There is no sign of foul play. It appears Mrs. McConnell voluntarily left Central Hospital upon learning of her husband's death, travelled to the top of Cathedral Ledge, and jumped off the edge to her death. It appears she committed suicide. We have no information as to why she chose to go to that location as opposed to some other location. I will take your questions."

Arthur Daniels, from one of the Boston area newspapers, raised his hand.

"Yes, Art. Go ahead." Rick responded.

The short, bald and bespectacled veteran reporter stood up to address the detective. His suit and tie looked as if they had time travelled from the 1940's into his closet. "And I guess it goes without saying, Detective, the likely reason for Mrs. McConnell's actions was her despondency over her husband's passing? I mean, the timing could hardly have been a coincidence, right?"

Rick looked at the reporter in silence for some time. The reporter found the delayed response quite odd. He'd considered his question to be of a routine and straight-forward nature. As he looked around the room at the other reporters, many of them seemed perplexed by the detective's slow reaction as well. Looking back towards the podium, Art awaited the answer.

Finally, Detective Earls replied in a guarded tone, "I agree the timing was not a coincidence."

Appearing uncomfortable, Rick scanned the room, looking over the reporters. "Any further questions?"

To Rick's surprise, the reporters remained quiet, confident they had the gist of the story.

"Alright, then," Rick concluded. "As stated, there is no evidence of foul play. The New Hampshire State Police will await the autopsy results on Mrs. McConnell. Absent any unexpected results, we will be closing the case, and this will be the last public statement we will be making with regard to it."

Winter Night

The surgery was going as planned for ear, nose and throat specialist Dr. John Russell this Friday afternoon. The patient needed a routine tonsillectomy. Things were well in hand, except that John was a little distracted. He and his fiancé has not been seeing eye to eye on a matter of great importance to him. At some point soon, he wanted to try to resolve it. As much as he tried to keep these thoughts and concerns at bay during work, and especially during surgery (routine or not), he found his mind drifting back to the rift he was having with her.

At the same time, in a different part of the city, Dr. Amy Cole was presiding over an operating room patient as well. An anesthesiologist, this surgery was not routine for her at all. The heart patient weighed 350 pounds. Under 275 was not a problem for her. Over that, however, things got a little dicey. It takes a lot of anesthesia to keep someone that heavy unconscious throughout the surgery. Administering too little ran the risk of having the patient wake up in the middle of the operation, but an overdose would be even more dangerous. Amy had decided to give a slightly lower dose than the charts indicated for a patient of this size, and then monitor his vital signs closely throughout the procedure. She was ready to increase the dose at the first sign of a problem.

About two thirds of the way through the procedure, she was caught off guard when the man's brain waves suddenly slowed to an alarmingly low level. Amy's pulse quickened and her face flushed as she tried to compose herself. Adding to an inadequate dose mid cut was one thing, reversing an overdose was quite another. If the problem didn't correct itself on its own- and fast- Amy wasn't certain she could bring him back. The image of the man's daughter, a teenager she had met in the visitor's room earlier, flashed before her eyes.

She let out a big sigh of relief under her mask when, after about seven seconds, the man's brain functioning returned to normal. She turned away from the monitor for a moment and glanced at the heart surgeon. He was in his fifties and had been practicing for about twenty five years. His opinion of the younger doctors, including Amy, carried some weight at the hospital. As best she could tell, he hadn't noticed the close call.

She was meeting her fiancé that evening for dinner in the North End, assuming neither of them got called into emergency service. The fatigue showed on her face as she tried to make her way through the crowded city streets around 6:30 p.m. It was winter in Boston and it was dark and cold. A strange feeling came to her out of the blue, something she couldn't put her finger on. Something important, she felt, was not right in her life. This feeling went away as quickly and mysteriously as it came, just as she entered the restaurant.

John, her fiancé, hadn't arrived yet. They had reservations, so she turned in her coat and sat in the lobby. She realized she'd forgotten to turn on her cell phone when she retrieved it from her locker after the surgery. She quickly reached into her pocket and turned it on. There was a message from her mother in Maryland.

She'd been waiting about twenty minutes when the doctor she was in love with arrived. Dr. John Russell was slender, six foot one and thirty two years old. The usual bright smile on her face upon seeing him was somewhat tempered as the rift between them was never totally out of mind. If they weren't planning on having children, it might not be as much of an issue, she thought. But they were planning on having children.

Amy was thirty years old. She was a five foot five brunette with blue eyes and a very bright smile. Ordinarily, she was a go getter type, a "type A" personality. In John's view, however, that seemed to have changed recently. He believed she was showing signs of mild depression, but he didn't mention that to her in a direct way. About a month earlier she had told him she was feeling down and she asked for his thoughts.

"You do believe in God, don't you? He's a good cure for the blues," he stated. She looked at him silently. This was something they had never discussed despite having dated for more than a year. "You're kidding, right?" she replied. She considered herself a scientist, and a good one at that. She thought the same of John, and looked up to him as a scientist. How could he believe such superstitions? Certainly, she was aware that some scientists professed to be religious. But she assumed much of it was political, a public front they used to appease family members and acquaintances, perhaps a way to network and fund raise. Surely most scientists didn't truly believe, deep down, in God.

But the look on her fiancé's face revealed, quite clearly, that he was not kidding. She was taken aback. She took a deep breath and then, treading lightly, replied, "Well, you're a scientist. I know you believe in evolution, and the two contradict each other, so how can you believe in God?"

"The two don't contradict each other. Science is a gift from God. Look, we were both raised Catholic. Remember the stories of Jesus healing the sick, then telling us to follow in his footsteps?" he asked. She looked at him quietly and nodded. Until now, she'd actually forgotten the stories of Jesus healing the sick. He continued, "That's why I went into medicine."

This was followed by a long silence during which the two simply stared at each other. She could not believe she was hearing him say these things. The thought crossed her mind that, perhaps, he wasn't the right man for her after all. Deep down, however, she knew he was. She was very drawn to him- emotionally, physically, and (she had thought) spiritually. She was dumbfounded at what she saw as his naïveté, and she couldn't believe what she was hearing.

"Well, that's not why I went into medicine," she replied, finally.

"That's right, I remember you said that you went into it because of what happened when you were a child," he offered.

"It's true, that is why I went into it," she confirmed.

What happened when she was a child was a near fatal bout of meningitis at age eight. Upon arriving at the hospital, the doctors looked her over and then told her parents, "We are not going to lie to you." Her parents were, of course, terrified as she slipped into a coma and remained so for nine days. The hospital did everything they could, but at some point it became a waiting game.

When Amy pulled through, her father was very grateful to the hospital's staff, as well he should have been. He always spoke very highly of doctors after that. Her mother, while appreciating what the hospital had done, seemed to have a different take on it, though it was never vocalized. Her mother seemed to change after Amy's close call, becoming quieter and more resigned. Sometimes Amy would happen upon her when she seemed to be meditating or, perhaps, silently praying. Once, her mother asked her what it had been like when she was in the coma. She wanted to know if Amy had seen or heard anything, "or anyone." Amy replied she didn't remember, because it was like being asleep.

"Oh, I see. But when people are asleep, they sometimes remember their dreams. Later on, I mean," her mother pointed out.

"I suppose so, mom," Amy acknowledged.

It was John's views, however, which caused their rift. For the past month, it had occasionally surfaced in conversation. Then it would go away, and then resurface. There were no angry debates, but there were brief conversations that seemed surreal to her. They were deeply in love, and both took the concept of binding to each other as soul mates in marriage seriously. This rift was something they had to either resolve or somehow work around.

But how could it be resolved? She didn't believe in God, it was as simple as that. True, she'd been raised a Catholic. As she grew up, however, she came to regard the whole phenomenon as hopelessly superstitious and disconnected from the reality of what was happening in the world.

She decided that she would let him have his say on the matter, but she wasn't going to rediscover Christianity or pretend that she did. The thorny question of how their children would be raised loomed on the horizon, but she didn't want to address it now.

She had calamari and red wine, while he had a more conventional plate of spaghetti and meatballs. They talked about how things had gone at work earlier on. She told him about the incident during the overweight man's surgery. "When it happened, when his brain waves slowed down so much, I thought for a second…" she had trouble getting the words out.

"You thought what?" John inquired, with some irony in his voice.

"Well, you know, we might lose him," she conceded.

John's apartment was a few blocks from the restaurant in the North End. It was in a quaint, stucco building with a courtyard in back, not far from the Old North Church and the statue of Paul Revere.

The couple ascended the stairs to the second floor apartment and sat across from each other at his kitchen table. "Listen, I know you don't want to talk about this and I'll never bring it up again if you listen to me tonight, unless we have children. I don't want to keep dragging this on forever either," he said.

Somewhat annoyed, she replied, "Fine, I'm listening." If he stuck to his word this would be a good thing, she felt. She'd listen to his speech, disregard it, and then they could move on. Many people with differing religious views have successful and happy marriages, she supposed.

John unbuttoned his sleeves and pulled them up. He was looking down at the table, not at her, and his forehead went into his hands. "I've never told anyone what I am about to tell you," he began. She was beginning to have that surreal feeling again as she looked at her fiancé. She felt that this was just a strange part of him she couldn't relate to.

"When I was twenty seven, I was living at a girlfriend's place…"

"You know I don't like to hear about your ex-girlfriends," she couldn't help but say.

"Well, this isn't really about her. Her place was near this cemetery. I mean, you could walk to it." He paused, and seemed to be struggling to find the words.

"Okay, yes, go on," she prodded.

"Well, we would sometimes walk to it and go for a jog in that cemetery. We'd start jogging at the entrance, and we'd go around twice and finish up close to where her mom was buried. Her mom died young." Amy was starting to become genuinely interested in the story. She found it odd that he was speaking so slowly and becoming emotional. "Well, anyway, this one night we finished our jog and I was resting on a stone wall near her mother's grave. She was praying at her mother's grave and was doing so for quite a while. At least it seemed that way to me. Then… what happened was…" Again, he was sputtering. He still hadn't looked up from the table. "What happened was, I saw this other grave nearby. It was one where you could tell the person's funeral just happened, because there were all these flowers around it. You know what I mean?" Upon asking that question, he finally looked up at her.

She smiled for a moment as she found humor in the question. "Yes, of course I've seen that before." She was watching him closely, more out of bewilderment than anything else, at this point.

"Well, I walked over to that grave while my ex was still praying at her mother's." He was looking down at the table again, his forehead back in his hands. "Kimberly White, it said. I didn't know who she was. But I kneeled down and started to pray for her. I asked God, in the name of Jesus Christ, to have mercy on her soul. I asked Him to let her into Heaven. Then I paused as questions started running through my head. "What if she hadn't been a good person? What if she'd done bad things, or was mean to people, or was selfish and made people miserable? Should I really be praying that she go to Heaven when I have no clue what kind of person she had been?" I thought about this for a few seconds, then addressed God again. "I don't care what she did or didn't do in her life. I am asking you, Lord, to let her into heaven anyway," I prayed. That was the end of the prayer.

He paused and took a sip of water. Amy hoped there was more to the story than that. Suddenly he looked up at her. She could tell by his face that there was, indeed, more to the story.

He reached across the table and took her hands into his. When he resumed the story, his voice started cracking from time to time. He was on the verge of tears, and she began to focus on him intensely.

"We slept at her place that night. In the middle of the night, I suddenly woke up out of a deep sleep. I mean, I woke right up all of the sudden. Okay?"

"Okay," she replied softly.

"Now, listen to me. Like I said, I have never told anyone this. I am not a crackpot, you know that. And I don't lie to you, you know that," he said, now looking her in the eyes. She knew those two statements were true. He was not a crackpot or a wacko and he had never lied to her. He continued, "As soon as I woke up, I saw someone at the foot of the bed, just standing there. I sat up immediately. I could see it was a woman and assumed it must have been my girlfriend. But I looked to my left and there was my girlfriend, sleeping. I remember looking at her lying there for an extra second or two, just to be sure. Then I looked back at the other person. I believed she had broken into the house and I was very alarmed. But it was the strangest thing, she was just standing there. She knew I had seen her, and she still just stood there." His voice cracked again. He wiped a tear from his eye, and then brought his hand back down to hers. He took a moment to regain his composure. Amy sat motionless as she listened.

"Clearly she had broken in, I thought. But she wasn't behaving as though she had broken in. And the fact that it was a woman was curious to me, as well. Plus, the way she was dressed was odd for a break in. She was wearing a white dress. She must have a male accomplice, I thought. I looked into the hallway, as the bedroom door was open. The hallway was totally quiet and undisturbed. I realized there was no one with her, she had come alone. I looked back and there she was, still in the same place and looking right at me. I'm telling you, the fact that she was there in that room was just as plain and clear to me that night as your presence in this room is right now. I no longer thought it was a robbery, however. I didn't know why she was there or what she wanted. I didn't know what I should say. Finally, I decided what to say. I decided to say, "Can I help you?" But just as the first word was about to come out of my mouth, just then, she disappeared. Just plain disappeared right in front of me."

Amy stared at him in stunned silence. She was feeling chills throughout her body. Suddenly, this felt *very* real to her. He looked back down at the table and his hands fastened onto hers more securely. His jaw was trembling and a tear rolled down his cheek. "I believe she came back, this Kimberly woman. I believe she had come back to thank me. I...I know she did." Just then, his hands rose up to cover his face as he began to sob.

Suddenly, Amy's face took on a new expression. Her face no longer seemed bewildered or skeptical. Hers was now a face of recollection. It was as if she'd suddenly remembered something she'd forgotten long ago, something that now had to be rekindled as soon as possible. Her eyes widened, her jaw dropped, and her hands rose from the table to cover her gaping mouth.

Low Tide

It was a Saturday morning in late September and temps were in the low 60's. Winter would come to this part of Maine soon, perhaps within a month. The summer crowds had once again left for the year and things had really slowed down. That was when Marissa liked this place best. Like many in her situation, she could be anywhere in the world right now. Travel was easy for her and money wasn't an issue.

Marissa stood on the wooden platform overlooking a dock just below where small boats were hitched. She had long black hair, very light skin, and she was quite tall. She was wearing a long white dress which, like her hair, flowed each time the cool breeze came off the water.

Marissa smiled as she watched an ordinary looking young man below her on the dock. There was no one else around the harbor this morning, it was just the two of them. He was not yet aware of her presence as he sat with his right foot in the salt water and his left foot flat on the dock. His left knee was pressed against his chin and his back was up against one of the dock's round support poles. It was clear that, like many boys his age, he was existentially bewildered. Moreover, like many boys his age, his hormonal emotions were unrequited and desperate. He was a local and not happy that the girls of summer had returned to Boston and New York.

All of this was evident to Marissa. She wondered how her memories might have been different if she had taken boys like him more seriously when she had the chance. Marissa had been born twenty years earlier and had grown up in Connecticut. She had been a girl of summer on Maine's coast. Her family maintained a second home in this very town, but they didn't come here anymore. For them, this was a place of sadness.

Marissa turned her head to the north and viewed the harbor at low tide. The peninsula extending from a small beach was barely visible due to the fog. The peninsula led to a long sandbar that stretched southward across the harbor such that it was parallel to where Marissa was standing. The sandbar would disappear at high tide each day. Somehow that made those who loved this place value it more. Marissa pulled herself away from the railing and left the platform.

Desperate- that is how Taylor viewed himself. Indeed, that was how he felt. Really desperate, and sex wasn't the half of it. Suicide was not out of the question. It wasn't imminent, or even likely, but it wasn't off the table, either. "It *can't* go on like this," he thought as his right foot swayed back and forth in the cool harbor. "Something has to change and change soon." He threw a rock into the harbor and watched it skip. He watched a bird swoop down and pluck a small fish right out of the water.

Taylor adjusted his position on the dock. Both feet were now in the water and he was facing the sandbar.

A fog rolling in from north to south obscured his view of the sandbar. Taylor vegged out as he looked at the fog rolling past. When it dissipated, he suddenly realized there was a tall brunette standing alone at the end of the sandbar. He had never seen her before. She was just standing there looking whimsically toward the south. He admired her long black hair and the beautiful white dress that caressed her from the ankles up. A familiar combination of heartache and happiness embraced him, amplified tenfold by where he was in his life's journey. A thirty year old man would have experienced the same feeling looking at Marissa, but with much less intensity than Taylor did.

Taylor's legs moved front and back as he gazed at the mysterious beauty. He watched as she swayed slightly as if the wind were blowing her.

Once again, a thick fog slowly rolled in. His eyes remained focused on her until, and even after, she disappeared in the fog. He did not want to look away. The fog thickened such that he could barely see his own hand if he were to hold it up to his face. His legs stilled in the harbor as the fog began to slowly clear out.

Taylor soon realized she was no longer there. He immediately looked northward, to his right, as he tried to locate her. After all, that was the only way in or out of that part of the sandbar, unless you wanted to swim. But she was nowhere to be seen. She was not on the sandbar, not on the peninsula, and not on the beach. She couldn't possibly have made it back to the mainland that quickly, Taylor realized. He looked back to the spot where she had been standing, as if she could have somehow reappeared there. He then looked at the water, to see if she had somehow fallen in or decided to go for an ill-advised swim in the cold September ocean. But again, nothing. No splashing or disturbances, the waters were completely calm.

Taylor stood up slowly, perplexed and alarmed. He was *certain* he had seen her. He was *certain* she had been there. He turned to his right and approached the decrepit wooden stairs that led to the upper platform. As he did, he saw something out of the corner of his right eye. He looked up to the platform and saw a light skinned young woman with deep blue eyes looking down at him. She did not look directly into his eyes, but her gaze was directed at him nonetheless. She had long dark hair, wore a long white dress, and was quite tall. She looked oddly familiar to him. When he reached the top, the young woman ran into his arms and held onto him tightly. As he was about to speak to her, she disappeared in his arms, leaving him holding nothing but air.

The Refugees

"Come here, Sparky, we're going in the house," Ruth called as she clapped her hands twice for her eight pound terrier. It was late September, 2008 in this remote part of Vermont, known locally as "The Northeast Kingdom." It was getting colder and darker earlier in the day now, and Ruth wanted to get inside. "Come now, Sparky, be a good boy."

The lake house, located deep in the woods and abutting a lake that isn't even on most maps, was vacated by its owners each winter. They were from Montreal, and Ruth knew they wouldn't be back until May. During the summer, Ruth squatted an A-frame style ski house near Burke Mountain, also in the Kingdom. The owners were from Boston and were only around on weekends from October through April. Ruth got away with it because she was smart about covering her tracks. She used minimal utilities so the owners wouldn't notice a sudden or large change in their monthly bills. She wrote down on paper exactly where things were in the respective houses when she arrived each season, and made sure everything was exactly as the owners had left it before she left and they returned. She always cleaned up after herself and the dog, leaving no trace of her presence. She had lies prepared in case she came across someone on the property and needed to explain herself.

"I'm Marcel's little sister, Marion. Do you know Marcel?" she once said to a meter reader. The owner's name was indeed Marcel, and he did have a younger sister, about Ruth's age, named Marion. Ruth had done her homework.

Of course, it was always possible the owners themselves could show up, off-season and unexpected. She had a story prepared for that as well. She would tell of a domestic violence crisis at her own house, and how she had just recently arrived and was hiding from the aggressor in the best way she could. She would apologize and promise to move out at once, but she hoped they would understand given the circumstances. She hadn't had to use that one yet, and she had been squatting for two years.

The dog settled in at his usual spot on the rug in the living room of the lake house. Ruth was eating beans out of a can and reading a book she had got at the library, sitting at the kitchen table. The kitchen was to the left upon entering through the front door of the house and was joined to the living room. Ruth could see Sparky from where she was sitting. The owner kept the house at forty five degrees in the winter to prevent the pipes from freezing. A backup generator would kick in in case the power ever went out. Ruth didn't know why he didn't drain the pipes and have no heat, but she was glad that he didn't. She turned it up to fifty, but no higher. On many winter nights, she and Sparky would huddle under a very thick sleeping bag Ruth owned.

When Ruth's psychiatrist had made a diagnosis of clinical depression, three years earlier, he stated in his report that Ruth most likely had the underlying gene which made her predisposed to that illness. Ruth's mother and great aunt had lived much of their adult lives with the illness. However, it was the rape which triggered the underlying susceptibility to mental illness and brought it to the surface, the doctor said. A second opinion confirmed the doctor's findings.

Two years prior to the doctor's diagnosis, at the age of twenty two, Ruth was forcibly raped by a stranger while jogging in a park near her parent's home in Northern New Hampshire. The man had never been identified or caught. After that, Ruth withdrew from the world.

At about nine p.m., as Ruth was continuing to read her book, a loud noise shook the back of the house. Ruth immediately went to the kitchen drawer and took out a steak knife. Sparky, all eight pounds of him, started growling and barking. Footsteps were heard coming down the hallway from one of the bedrooms at the back of the house, and the hallway light had been turned on. Somehow, someone had breached one of the windows in the bedroom from the outside. Although Ruth had a knife in her hand, she wasn't about to scare anyone. She seemed paralyzed against the kitchen counter near the sink.

A man appeared from the hallway. Ruth was terrified. She could barely discern his features as only one light in the kitchen was on and it was directly above his head. She could see that he was quite tall and thin.

"Woa," he began. "I'm sorry, I thought this house was unoccupied." He looked down and saw the knife in her hand. She remained silent. Sparky was barking, growling and biting at the man's ankles. The man hardly noticed. He looked at her suspiciously. "Do you…" then he paused. He looked into her face but did not approach. He thought she was pretty, but also realized that there was something off about her - something wrong. "Do you own this place?"

Sparky continued gnawing wildly on the man's pants. His eyes glanced down at the dog for a second and then immediately returned to the woman with the steak knife. She did not answer him. "Look, I don't think you own this place. These look like summer homes, owned by upper class out of towners. I'm pretty sure you are squatting here, aren't you?" Again he gazed at her, waiting for a response or an answer that did not come. "I'm not trying to make trouble," he continued as he knelt down and patted Sparky even while Sparky continued to attack. He wasn't especially worried about Ruth's knife because he had a loaded hand gun in his jacket pocket.

"I just need to sleep here tonight and I'll be gone in the morning. I won't tell anyone your secret. Just let me sleep here tonight and I'll be gone. No problems, Okay?" But Ruth still didn't respond, verbally or non-verbally. Her grip on the knife tightened. "What are you, a deaf mute?" he said, his voice louder.

"No, I'm not," she retorted immediately. He stood up again and looked at her, his head starting to nod slowly. He seemed to be sizing her up. Sparky went silent and walked back to his usual place on the rug.

"Oh, I get it," he stated, knowingly. "You're a victim of some type, like everybody else in this country. So you're free-loading off others and won't talk to anybody, is that it?"

She looked at him silently. He was an asshole, but probably not dangerous, she concluded. "Well, just don't stab me in my sleep in the name of self defense, keep that mutt away from me, and we'll get through the night. Got it?" he continued.

"Why do you need to sleep here tonight?" she challenged, loosening her grip on the knife.

"I've got my reasons," he replied, somewhat more humbly.

"Well, you can't sleep in the bedroom on the owner's bed. I want things left *exactly* as I found them. You can sleep in that room to your right, behind you. You can sleep on the floor, it has wall to wall carpeting," she asserted. She was referring to a room the owners used as a sort of play room for their children.

"Fair enough. I have a sleeping bag with me, so it should work out fine," he assented. "Remember, no trouble, I'm just crashing here tonight and leaving in the morning, first thing. By the way, my name's Mark." They stood there looking at each other for about twenty seconds. Ruth put the knife down on the counter and folded her arms.

"I'm Ruth," she countered. The man gathered his belongings and entered his room for the night.

Like Ruth, Mark was twenty seven years old. He was six foot and one inch tall, in good physical condition and had a rugged sort of handsomeness about him. He was a deserter from the Army, and was currently classified as AWOL. The authorities were looking for him. Originally from Maine, he was on his way to Canada. His plan was to attempt a border crossing into Quebec province the next day. He was traveling by bicycle, so as not to be traced by a license plate. He had served one tour of duty each in Iraq and Afghanistan. The military told him in August that he had to go back to Iraq. He did not want to go back.

It had been a long day for Mark, as he had traveled a great distance on his bike. He had been doing so for ten days with a minimal but still cumbersome stash of belongings in his backpack. Now he was only twenty two miles from the Canadian border.

With his sleeping bag laid out on the floor of the play room, he fell fast asleep at around nine thirty.

Ruth continued reading while Sparky dozed off on the rug. Ruth had planned on turning in about eleven o'clock. But at about ten fifteen, she heard loud yelling in the play room. She couldn't make out the words, but she figured the outburst was due to a nightmare. She continued reading. Seven or eight minutes later she heard screaming, louder this time.

Disturbed, Ruth put the book down and stood up slowly from the chair. The door to the play room was slightly ajar. Slowly, *very slowly,* Ruth approached. As she got closer, another incomprehensible outburst stopped her in her tracks. If his shouts were in a language, it wasn't English.

Ruth resumed her slow advance toward the doorway. She was shaking, but there was more to that than a fear for her personal safety. His yelps were harrowing, more so in these otherwise silent and wooded surroundings.

Ruth reached the doorway with her arms tightly folded in front of her. Her foot gently pushed the door open enough for her to get a good look at him. He was silent at the moment, but he was also shaking noticeably. She leaned against the casing of the doorway. She could see his face clearly despite the dim lighting, and for a moment she allowed herself to admire it. Suddenly he writhed about violently and screamed ferociously, startling Ruth. The scream was followed by a lengthy rant, as though he were yelling directives at someone who wasn't listening. Again, the words made no sense.

Ruth was trembling against the casing of the doorway. She had no idea what this was about. Clearly, it was more than an ordinary nightmare. Something had happened to him once, something very bad. His earlier bravado was a front for a very vulnerable person, she realized.

Her arms remained folded. She eased away from the casing of the doorway. Her right foot, bare, advanced into the play room slowly. It came to rest on the rug. Her left foot was still in the doorway. Then his rant got louder. Ruth slowly moved her right foot back into the doorway, and again leaned up against the casing. At no time did she take her eyes off him.

Suddenly, she heard something behind her. She realized that Sparky was charging the doorway. She turned around quickly and grabbed him before he could enter the room. "No, no, Sparky, it's Okay, go back to sleep," she whispered, but to no avail. Sparky was excited and barking. She placed Sparky on the floor of the living room and quickly stepped backward into the play room. She immediately shut the door, keeping Sparky out, as she didn't want him to wake the traveler up. Sparky's barks were barely audible when the door was shut.

At that point, Ruth was inside the play room with Mark and the door was closed. The only light was provided by a moon ray through a small window in the top left corner of the room. As her eyes adjusted, a very loud outburst (the loudest yet) escaped Mark and shook Ruth. She immediately ran to him and laid herself down beside him to his right. She wrapped her arms around his shoulders and brought her face close to his as he shook uncontrollably.

"Shhh…Shhh…" she whispered into his ear. "It's Okay, it's just a dream. I'm here, it's Okay" She was acting on instinct at this point. She had abandoned calculated decision making. "Shhh.. .Shhh…" she went on, kissing his cheek softly. Still asleep, he calmed down immediately.

He was quiet and mostly still for a while after that. She unzipped his sleeping bag and crawled into it with him, now on his left side. She placed her head and left arm on his chest, and faded into sleep herself.

They stayed like that for a couple of hours, both sleeping peacefully in each other's arms. Mark had moments of lucidity during this time, when he would be semi conscious but still not fully aware or awake. He knew there was a woman lying with him, but didn't question it. Once, he believed he was still married and she was his (then) wife. A while later, he figured he must have gone to a bar and picked up a woman (perhaps back in Maine.) Still later, he thought it was a nurse he had desired after being injured by shrapnel in Afghanistan.

But by one thirty a.m., he was back into a deep state of sleep again. Ruth was in a deep sleep as well, unaware that she had a man in her arms. But then, suddenly, her whole body was jerked to the left and back to the right violently like a rag doll. A blood curdling scream pierced her ears and she awakened again to the situation. Although very frightened, she did not consider getting up and leaving him. She grabbed his shirt tightly with both hands, holding on like a child to a safety bar on a roller coaster. She positioned her head in the middle of his chest so as to minimize risk of a head injury. His violent gyrations continued and his verbal outburst got louder. She tightened her grip more. When she could get a word in, she tried her best to soothe him with her voice and caresses. This time it took longer to bring him down, but her persistence paid off. His physical spasms decreased slowly and eventually stopped. He slowly quieted down as well.

"It's Okay, I'm here. I'm not leaving. I'm not leaving. Shhh…Shhh…" she whispered.

After a few minutes, they both faded into a relaxed sleep again, and remained that way for hours. At some point before sunrise, Ruth had turned over such that she was a few feet to his left, and was sleeping on the bare rug outside of the sleeping bag.

Sunlight from the room's lone window crossed Mark's face. It was six a.m. Gradually, Mark arose from his slumber. He sat up in his sleeping bag and ran his hands over his face. He glanced to his left and was startled to see her there, sleeping. He realized the squatter had spent the night with him. He was vaguely aware of the fact that her presence had been comforting to him during the night, though he had no specific recollections.

He quietly gathered his belongings, not wanting to wake her. Once he had everything, he opened the door to enter the living room. He saw Sparky sleeping on the rug. He stopped for a moment in the doorway and looked back at the squatter, asleep on the floor. He noticed that she was lying flat on her back. Her feet were together and pointing downward. Her arms were outstretched horizontally on the floor. Her head was bowed slightly to the right.

Mark walked towards her quietly and knelt down beside her. He kissed her cheek gently, then her forehead. He noticed she was perspiring a little. He opened one of his bags and took out a clean, white face cloth. He gently placed it over her face and wiped away the moisture, being careful not to wake her. She was breathing quietly and looked comfortable as he admired her face. Putting the cloth back in his bag, he quietly left the lake house and headed north.

When Ruth awakened, she made her way to the kitchen table and sat there silently for some time, gathering her thoughts. She then packed up her belongings into her two suit cases. She dialed her mother on her Trac Fone as she picked up around the house. "Mom, can you come get Sparky and I in Vermont? I'm ready to come home now."

The Masterpiece

"What you are looking for is 'significant form'. Does this work of art cause an emotional response of some magnitude. It doesn't necessarily matter what the response is. It can be sadness, anger, joy… whatever, but it's got to do something for you emotionally to have significant form," said the bespectacled, middle aged instructor as he looked over the class. As usual, Ethan (in the front row) seemed perplexed.

"Go ahead, Ethan," the balding instructor said with some reluctance.

"Well, for a lot of people, myself included, there has to be some realism in the picture to stir an emotion. It has to look like something in the real world. You know, like a mountain or a lake or a building… *something*. But these paintings just don't look like anything real."

The instructor replied, "They're not supposed to. Real objects don't contribute to significant form. They don't subtract from it, but they don't add to it, either. They're excess baggage. All I can tell you, Ethan, is you'll need to see that for yourself at some point if you're ever going to understand abstract art."

Ethan was a twenty six year old social worker in Western Massachusetts. For reasons his girlfriend Julia found mysterious, he was pursuing an associate's degree in Art History by taking classes at night. Abstract Art, which he simply didn't "get", was a required course he was unhappy about having to take. He vented to Julia about it as they lay in bed after he got home that night.

"Excess baggage. That's what he called real stuff. *Excess baggage.* I just don't get it. Those random patterns and lines and images, who can be 'stirred' by such things? The don't stir up memories in anybody, not the way a real object would, anyhow."

Julia rolled her eyes as she lay on her side, facing the other way. "Every time you come back from that abstract class, you start ranting about it. I think you should just do what you have to to pass and then you can forget about the abstractionists, or whatever they're called. They're just a bunch of weirdos, anyway."

He had viewed at length a number of abstract works from the big names (de Stael, Delaunay, Severini, Picasso and so on). But none of it "clicked" for him. He was like the hapless philosopher trying to "get" existentialism.

"What is your monthly income?" Ethan inquired of the young woman bouncing a toddler on her knee as she sat in his office. "How much was your heat bill last year…do you get a federal subsidy for rent…how is the child insured…" He typed all of her answers. He filled in the boxes. "Okay, you qualify for heat assistance. You'll get $800.00 this year," he advised. "Do you have any questions?"

"Nope," she replied, putting the toddler's hat on his head.

"This Noland painting, to me, does have significant form," the lecture began. This was the first time the instructor did not have his glasses on. Apparently, he did own contact lenses. "It creates a sense of chaos by using jarring and asymmetrical angles. It stirs anxiety in the viewer. Anxiety is an emotion. This work is a reminder that many things in life are not as they seem." Ethan sat in the front row, slowly shaking his head back and forth.

"If you start in with *that* again, you're sleeping on the couch tonight," Julia informed him as she curled up on the sofa to watch TV, arms folded. Ethan opened the refrigerator and pulled out an I. P.A.

The semester winded down and only the final exam remained. The abstract art exam was scheduled for a Wednesday night in mid- December. All the lectures had been given, and Ethan was no closer to having the elusive knack for identifying the holy grail of "significant form" than he had been the first day of the semester. How could anyone say with authority that one piece of abstract art was a masterpiece while another was a piece of junk? Ethan knew he couldn't.

The morning of the exam, a woman appeared in his office with her daughter. The girl was perhaps four or five years of age. As the appointment began and he started asking the woman questions, the girl looked straight at Ethan without interruption for longer than what could be considered normal. This was making him a little uncomfortable. Soon the girl began a repeated chant of gibberish or, perhaps, a language besides English. Either way, Ethan didn't understand what she was saying. Yet she repeated the chant, saying the same thing over and over, louder each time.

"Worsh hail bur stumpick," it went. "*WORSH HAIL BUR STUMPICK!!!*" she continued, as though demanding a reply from him.

"She's autistic," the mother offered, explaining the situation.

"Oh, I see," he said. "How old is she?"

"She's four," the woman answered, with a proud smile on her face as she looked at her daughter, her treasure.

Just then, the girl quieted down and started doodling on a piece of paper as Ethan refocused on the task at hand. "How did your husband become unemployed..."

The girl ran from Ethan's desk to the room's window, looked out of it, and returned to the desk. She doodled some more, ran back to the same window and looked out, returned to the desk again and so on.

As the interview wrapped up, Ethan asked if the woman had any questions. She did not. She packed up her belongings and left with the girl, into the cold New England winter.

Ethan started cleaning up his desk, organizing the client's signed documents and so on. The specter of the evening's exam reentered his mind and troubled him as he decluttered his work space. To his left, he noticed the autistic girl's scribbled sheet of paper near the stapler. She had apparently forgotten it and left it behind. Ethan picked it up with the intention of disposing of it and moving onto his next task. Just as his free hand approached the document to crumple it up, he froze. Something about it had caught his eye, and he couldn't seem to turn his gaze from it. He was like a deer in the headlights. To him, the long and slanted lines across the plain, white background resembled a monsoon rainstorm, a waterfall, or something of that nature. It was beautiful, even breathtaking. As he continued admiring it, he realized it was not a drawing of torrential rains or a waterfall in a conventional sense. Someone like Julia might very well see something else entirely (stands of spaghetti, perhaps?) Or she might see just scribbled lines. A lump traveled up and down Ethan's throat as he let go of the document and sat back in his chair. "Wow," he said, as he looked at the wall and stared "into space".

A Kingdom Greater
than Rome

I. OCTOBER 28, 1982
HANOVER, NEW HAMPSHIRE

Laura was already in her pajamas as her roommate studied at
a desk. "I know it's early, but I'm going to bed, I'm just really
tired all of the sudden. It sort of came over me in the last hour
or so." Denise, her roommate, did not look up from her text
book. "It happens," she opined and then paused. Something
in the textbook had caught her attention. Eventually, Denise
continued, "I'll be up for a while yet. Hopefully the light won't
bother you. I've got a big physics test tomorrow."

Laura said her prayers silently and then drifted off to sleep
very quickly. It was only 8:30 p. m., about three hours prior to
her usual bedtime. She was part of the Dartmouth Crew Team,
and the early practices had finally caught up with her. The light
from Denise's desk didn't bother her, at least not for very long.

Denise was focused like a laser beam on her physics textbook. She aspired to be a science teacher, and perhaps even
a college professor one day. She took her studies seriously.
Laura was a supportive and cooperative roommate, whom

she had known just over a year. They were sophomores and had requested each other as roommates after each had had a fairly challenging experience as freshman. Denise was from Philadelphia, while Laura hailed from Boston. The ferocious Celtics-Sixers rivalry at the time was the only thing the girls seemed to be at odds about.

At 10:45 p. m., Denise quickly turned from her textbook and looked directly at Laura.

Light was all around Laura. Beautiful, transcendent light, unlike anything Laura had ever seen. The light was in front of her, behind her, above and below her. Laura had never felt so warm, yet she was not uncomfortable. On the contrary, she was perfectly comfortable. In addition, she felt cared for and cared about. She could feel her presence moving through the light and into brighter light. The warmth was like a hot tub without water, and then there were the images. Beautiful, breathtaking images glided before her. Laura took in as much as she could. Colors she had never seen, or even imagined, appeared before her. A kalidescope of strange and unforgettable beauty awed her. She was an observer and a passive recipient of what she was experiencing, the likes of which she had never conceived of in her wildest and most optimistic dreams.

Her sensation of gliding, however, stopped abruptly when she encountered a female entity of some sort before her. She could only see the entity's "head," as its entire body was concealed by a white garment or sheet, it seemed. Laura could only conclude this entity was an angel. Its eyes sparkled like a pond on a very sunny day. Its smile was a radiant beam that seemed to go through Laura as she marveled at it. Its hair glowed with extreme brightness.

At one point, Laura felt as if this angel had embraced her. The closest thing Laura could compare this embrace to was a "hug," but it wasn't really a hug. Instead, Laura felt completely engulfed by the embrace, and she realized this angel – this glittering angel – loved her in a way she had never experienced before. After the embrace, Laura gazed at her brilliant and glowing beauty for some time. Whatever worldly concerns or worries she had a few hours earlier were long, long gone.

After a while, Laura felt a male presence address her. The human or earthly equivalent of this this exchange would be like a mentoring or fatherly man placing his hand on a young woman's shoulder in order to guide her in a particular direction. Laura felt herself turning back, away from the angel. She realized that God was leading her back, most likely to where she had come from. She didn't want to go back, but had no say in the matter. She had been turned around and was gliding back, away from the light and warmth.

"Laura, Laura, can you hear me?"

Laura opened her eyes. Three people in medical garments surrounded her. "Laura, you are at Dartmouth Hospital. Your roommate called an ambulance when you went into convulsions and stopped breathing. You had an aneurysm, Laura. It is highly unusual for someone your age, but it can happen."

Laura looked at the doctor with a hazy, glassy eyed look on her face. She was absorbing some of what the woman was saying, but not all of it. Her eyes wondered to the corner of the room where she noticed her boyfriend Scott standing. Scott somehow looked different to her than she had remembered him.

II. DECEMBER 16, 1986
     BOSTON, MASSACHUSETTS

Laura held her mother's hand at the bedside, where she had been for two and a half hours. "Yes, Mom, the nurse will be here soon. She said she will bring water. Do you want me to get another pillow for you?"

Scott, Laura's husband, stood against the wall. He wanted to give Laura some space to be with her mother, Edith. There wasn't much time left for his mother in law, who was dying with pancreatic cancer.

"I'm scared," Edith said to her daughter with a look of profound sadness on her face. Laura looked back at her mother for some time. She seemed to be searching her mother's face for something, something she wasn't finding. She seemed to be at an impasse, unsure of what to say or how to respond. She looked down towards the floor, swallowed, and tightened her grip on her mother's hand. Edith remained focused on her daughter, hoping for a response that would somehow put her at ease.

"Mom," Laura began, still looking at the floor, "You have nothing to worry about." She paused for a few moments. Then she looked up at her mother and repeated her statement, matter of factly. "You have nothing to worry about. Mom, I'm going to tell you something I have never told anyone. Listen to me, I have something to tell you."

Laura's facial expressions, movements, and the tone of her voice revealed how emotional she was becoming. She was struggling to put the words together in her mind.

Scott, previously detached from the discussion, was now very focused on his wife. This thing she had referred to, was it really something she had never told anyone? Never told him? What's more, he had never seen her quite like this before. Her demeanor was very humble now, almost childlike.

"Mom, do you remember when I was in college, and they rushed me to the hospital one night? My roommate called the ambulance and they revived me at the hospital. Do you remember?"

"Yes," Edith replied. "Of course I remember."

"Well," Laura continued, "before I came through, something happened. Something I never told anyone about."

Scott remembered the night in question well. Prior to that night, he wasn't sure if Laura was the one for him or not. She had good qualities, but she was also uptight and high strung. After that night, she became much more mellow and at ease. Scott had always assumed there was a medical reason for the change, especially given the neurological cause of the emergency. He stood motionless now, hanging on his wife's every word. It was as if the two women had forgotten he was there, and he was eaves-dropping on a private conversation. Whatever was coming next, it would indeed be the first time he had heard it as well.

"Mom, I felt very warm but comfortable. Warmth was all around me and going through me. There was a soft, pleasant light all around me as well. This went on for some time. I had never experienced anything like it. After a while I could see beautiful colors, not like earthly colors, but strange and indescribable colors that seemed to glide by in slow waves. One of the colors, I guess, was comparable to blue but it wasn't really blue. Like I say, I couldn't put a name on it or even describe it," she continued. She paused and took a deep breath. She was becoming very emotional, and seemed to struggle to find the words she wanted to say next. Scott saw a lump rise and descend in her throat. She was looking down at the floor again, and her hands were rubbing both of her knees as her body moved slowly back and forth in her chair. If a world existed outside of this hospital room, Scott was barely aware of it at that moment.

Laura looked up at her mother. Edith had at most days, and possibly mere hours, left. She looked back at Laura, gazing directly into her daughter's eyes.

"I then saw a young woman, or something like a woman, anyway," Laura continued. "I could only see her from the neck up, her body was covered by something white. It was sort of like a sheet, but not exactly. I can't really say what it was. She stood right in front of me, and something was behind her. It was some sort of *realm*. I couldn't 'see' it, exactly, but I knew it was there and I wanted to enter it and never leave it. I knew, somehow, that this realm was a place where blind people could see and deaf people could hear. I knew those things about this realm. But there was something about the girl, as well. Something needing to be dealt with or resolved first. She smiled at me and her eyes sparkled. I mean, *really* sparkled."

Laura paused and took several deep breaths in a row. She was becoming short of breath, it seemed. She did not look down this time, her eyes remained fixed on her mother.

"Her hair had this extreme brightness and glow to it. I had never seen anything or anyone like her…"

Laura's voice was starting to crack. Scott noticed a tear rolling down her left cheek.

"She was the most beautiful creature I had ever seen. I… well…I… I loved her," Laura concluded, barely able to finish vocalizing her thoughts. She became quiet, but tears were now streaming down her both sides of her face.

Edith seemed entranced by what her daughter was saying. She had a question, "Did you know who she was? I mean, did you recognize her? Could she have been your Aunt Cathy?"

Laura regained some of her composure. "I don't think it was Aunt Cathy, mom. I have thought about that over the last few years, but I don't think it was her. I didn't recognize her, mom, but it was the strangest thing. I did seem to know her, somehow. I mean, not by name. She wasn't someone I'd ever met before, but I still felt as if I knew her. I can't really explain it. Anyway, I felt God's presence – yes, I know it was God – I felt His presence start to guide me back in the other direction, the direction I had come from. I was not allowed to look at or see God, but I was allowed to sense his presence. It was like

He had his hand on my shoulder even though there weren't really hands or shoulders in this place. I didn't want to leave but I knew I had to. I knew God wanted me to and I knew it had something to do with the girl I saw, the angel."

Scott had not moved an inch in the last several minutes. He had been utterly engrossed by his wife's revelation. He felt a twinge of jealousy in the sense that this angel had played such a large role in Laura's existential reality, but that was not his primary response to his wife's astounding confession. He had always been a spiritual person in his own right. He was fascinated and intensely curious about the girl – the angel, it seemed – who had moved Laura so deeply. Who was she? And why had she delayed Laura's entrance to the Kingdom?

III.   MAY 18, 2012
       AMHERST, MASSACHUSETTS

Laura and Scott sat on the fold up chairs along with the other proud parents. They were waiting for their daughter's name to be called. It wouldn't be long now, they knew. Laura placed her hand into her husband's, clasping her fingers between his. Most of the graduates crossing the stage were wearing black caps and gowns, but the nursing school graduates had decided to go with their traditional white uniforms. Finally, Laura heard her daughter Jessica's name called.

An only child, Jessica had made her parents proud by choosing a healing profession and by taking her studies seriously. She already had a job offer from a Boston Hospital. She was twenty two years old.

Jessica walked across the stage in her white nurse's uniform. After taking her diploma, she looked towards the crowd in the general direction of her parents. A free spirit, she decided to throw her cap in the air right then and there, instead of waiting until the end of the ceremony when the others would. So she flung the cap high in the air, as her long blond hair loosened and began blowing in the wind. It was a very sunny day, and her hair shined in the sunlight brilliantly. She was joyous at having finally received the degree she had worked hard for. As she looked toward her parents, she beamed with a smile from ear to ear, and her eyes sparkled in the sunlight.

Socialized

Crystal Lake held a seven point lead over Wooden Hills with less than one minute remaining. Crystal Lake had led throughout much of the game as their star point guard, Bobby Whitaker, had scored a team high twenty one points. He was now dribbling away, trying to run out the clock, so that Wooden Hills would have no choice but to foul him. The opponents complied, and Bobby promptly hit two free throws, extending his team's lead to nine points with less than thirty seconds remaining.

A short while later, the buzzer sounded, and Crystal Lake had won their tenth game in a row. Excited, the high school boys started to festively high five each other and otherwise celebrate. "Nice job, kids! Ten in a row, I'm very proud of you!" shouted John Wilson, Crystal Lake's head coach. Their six foot center, Jimmy Bradley, seemed particularly enthused. His arms were raised and he shouted something about ripping the nets down with his bare hands. In the middle of the revelry, forward Ricky Jones suddenly stopped celebrating. He had noticed the team's other forward, Andy Shields, was just sitting on the bench and had apparently not left it. Andy was usually the first to celebrate a win, so Ricky was perplexed. He walked over to the bench and looked down at his somber teammate.

"What's up? Why aren't you celebrating with us? Didn't you notice we won the game? One more win and we clinch a…"

"Look at them," Andy replied, pointing towards the Wooden Hills side of the court. Ricky turned towards his left. What about the losing team could have distracted his teammate so? He was curious. At first, Ricky didn't notice anything out of the ordinary, but the more he looked, the more unsettled he became. He took a seat next to Andy, without taking his eyes off the Wooden Hills' players.

"Okay kids, a few more high fives. Now make the 'v' sign for victory with your fingers. Hold them right up," Coach Taylor of Wooden Hills instructed. Turning his attention to the cheerleaders, the coach then inquired, "Did you get that shot, girls? Keep snapping those phones. Don't post to Facebook or Snapchat yet, we'll do that later, just keep clicking for now. We want some good ones. You know the drill."

"What the hell are they doing?" Andy wondered aloud, turning his attention to Ricky. By now, a couple of other Crystal Lake players had wandered over and were standing near Ricky and Andy. They too were watching the Wooden Hills players, with their hands on their hips.

"They seem to be genuinely happy and joyful," Ricky observed. "As if they really believe they won the game."

Suddenly questioning reality, as well as his own sanity, Andy looked up at the scoreboard again. *Didn't we just beat them?* he wondered. Sure enough, the scoreboard read, "Crystal Lake 57, Wooden Hills 48." Indeed, what the heck was going on?

"Okay, team photo, everybody huddle up. All smiles now, you hear? I want all or your right fists in the air, all except Sean. You kneel down in the middle and hold the basketball up with both hands," continued Wooden Hills' Coach Taylor. "All right, girls, come over here with those cell phones and start snapping, we'll post to the internet later."

"Can you believe this guy?" Coach Wilson of Crystal Lake said to one of his assistant coaches. He then took a deep breath before continuing. "I had heard a rumor about this team. I had heard that they do this after every game, win or lose, at the direction of their coach. I didn't believe it until now…until I saw it. Supposedly, he justifies this crap by saying it's all about 'positive thinking.' Nothing else matters except that. 'Positive thinking.' What kind of lesson is he teaching these kids, anyway? What a jackass. Is this really what life in the 21ˢᵗ Century has come to?"

After the teams retreated to their locker rooms, Coach Taylor addressed the Wooden Hills' players. "Listen, there are some things we can improve on. Too many times I see you guys shooting the ball from outside when there's an open guy underneath. Remember, look for the open man, there's no need to rush the shot. Now, let's do the locker room selfie. Huddle up."

Joe Wilcox, an assistant coach, handed Coach Taylor their ever present poster board sign, which read, "ANOTHER WIN FOR WOODEN HILLS!" Placing the poster board in the hands of Sean Gray, who was again kneeling in front of the huddled team, Coach Taylor joined the huddle, smiling broadly. Joe Wilcox focused his cell phone on the team. "Make the victory sign and smile!" he said, as he snapped and snapped and snapped.

Higher

I.

"Now boarding Flight 957 non stop to New York at gate 22…"

Grace started getting her carry-ons together, motioning to her six year old daughter, Laura, it was time to go. She presented two tickets to the man at gate 22. Grace was a biology professor at Berkeley. She was headed to New York to visit her dad, who was in failing health. She'd grown up in New York, but returned less and less in recent years. She had been fixated on her work, trying to develop a vaccine for Dengue Fever and other viruses common in the third world.

"I bet dad will forget to feed Boots," Laura opined. Her arms were folded across her chest and she had a scowl on her face as she sat in the window seat of the plane. Boots was their cat.

"No, honey, we'll call to remind him. Boots will be fine."

"I'm definitely going to call to remind him," Laura's arms were still folded. "What are those people doing with their hands?" Laura pointed to a woman and a child who had just boarded.

"Well, I think that the boy must be deaf. He can't hear anything, so they talk to each other with their hands. You should pray for him tonight," Grace replied as she took a sip of water.

Laura still had a scowl on her face. "I will, but at least he has hands. If he didn't have any hands and he was deaf, then he couldn't talk at all."

Grace took another sip of water before responding, "I suppose your right, honey."

II.

"I swear I would ram this guy in front of me if I wasn't running late for that plane," Karl fumed.

"I am starting to get worried, too," Tracy, his mistress, concurred as she looked at her watch. "We shouldn't have boozed so hard last night, we're going to miss this plane," she continued.

"Look, doll. I closed a huge deal yesterday. We're talking big bucks, huge money. I got what I came out here for. The boys on the street (Wall Street) will be impressed, no doubt about it. They didn't think I could pull it off."

She kissed the side of his face. "I know, baby. You told me all about it last night. You think I don't listen, but I remember all about those lockup clauses you talked about, so the other side can't back out of the deal and all, not without having to pay millions, anyway. You kept saying it was great to have a piece of the derivatives market, and so on. But it wasn't until your fourth drink that you started paying attention to *my* assets. I was starting to feel slighted." She looked at him with a coy smile. He slammed on the horn at the car in front of him, even though it was bumper to bumper traffic and there was no place for the other driver to move to.

"I've decided that I really don't like Frisco," Tracy continued. "Too many weirdos. Too many granola, hippie types.

I want to get back to Manhattan and I don't want to have to schedule a later flight. We're on Flight 957, I've got the tickets right here. We're never going to make it, Karl, never."

III.

The deaf boy's companion was not, in fact, his mother. The boy's hearing loss was a result of a car crash that killed both of his parents when he was only four years old. He was now eight. His companion, Maria, was a twenty eight year old special needs teacher who'd been working with him at a boarding school for the deaf in Oakland since soon after the accident. His best rapport was with her and he was making a lot of progress. Sign language was only one of the exceptional talents Maria had for working with special needs children.

At present, she was fulfilling the boy's dream of going to New York City. He often signed about the Empire State Building and his desire to go to the top. It took some doing, but Maria had persuaded the school's principle to approve the trip. Maria was even fronting some of the expenses herself. The two sat quietly as they waited for takeoff. After fastening her seat belt and getting herself situated, Maria looked over at the boy. He had a big smile and look of wonder on his face.

IV.

"You sure you're O.K., Jim?"

The Chairman of the Board, Mr. Drake, looked to his left and responded, "Yes, Mike, I'll be alright. I want to wrap this meeting up by 9:30. My plane leaves at, let me see here..." Jim pulled out his wallet and found his plane ticket. "It's Flight 957 and it leaves at noon. I'll be back in New York by nine or ten tonight, Eastern Time. I'll be O.K. once I'm back in New York. My wife knows what to give me for the aches and pains."

The meeting convened. Jim Drake was also CEO of the company and he wanted updates from the headquarters of the subsidiary company he had annexed by hostile takeover the year before. Often, he would simply call, e-mail, or teleconference from his office in New York, but the matters under discussion at this meeting were "too sensitive" to risk an electronic record.

"These financial statements show a debt to equity ratio that seems high, historically speaking. I'm concerned about raising the regulators' red flag…" Jim began. He looked at the others around the table for a reaction.

There was a pause. Finally, the vice president of the subsidiary company spoke, "We are not concerned about regulators," he said.

Jim raised his eye brow. "Why not?"

"Well, things have changed, Jim. It's not like it was back in the nineties. Regulators really have no power. We can do anything we want."

Jim winced, as he felt a sharp pain in his stomach. He didn't understand it. He had woke up this morning in his hotel room with pain in both his stomach and his back. There had been no prior symptoms.

"I understand regulators have been cut down to size over the last ten or twelve years, but they did get some teeth back after the crash in 2008." Jim positioned himself in his chair for greater comfort.

Another member of the board, a woman in her early forties, spoke up. "We've looked into it. They had teeth for a little while after the crash, maybe a year or so, but then similar companies started leveraging heavily again and they were getting away with it. When you have the kind of size and capital we have, you can do as you like."

Jim looked at the lady, admiring her features for a moment. He couldn't tell exactly what color her eyes were. They were either green or hazel.

"Well then," Jim replied, "Seems like you folks have that angle covered. What's going on with tax abatement?" Again, there was a pause. Jim was fifty seven years old and sometimes got the sense that the younger players considered him out of touch.

Again the vice president, a man in his late forties, spoke up. "Our accountants and lawyers have been working on it, sir. I have with me a report that outlines how we can reduce our tax liability to zero."

Jim appeared taken aback. "Zero? Let me see that report."

The vice president slid the binder on the table towards Jim. Jim reached for it and groaned loudly as the pain in his back resurfaced.

"My goodness, Mr. Drake. Are you certain that you're O.K.?" the woman offered.

"I'm not certain, bear with me and I should get through this." Jim perused the report. "These shelters and loopholes appear to meet legal and accounting requirements. This is some good arbitrage you folks have put together here. Most impressive, give my compliments to your team."

The vice president smiled, "Thank you, sir." The vice president was trying to move the meeting along. Whatever might be happening with Mr. Drake, medically speaking, he didn't want it to happen here at his office complex.

Jim continued, "However, from a P. R. standpoint, I'm a little concerned about zero. What if the media somehow got hold of that? I know, we could wait for the story to die down and then change the name of the company when the public is no longer looking, but that's a pain in the ass. Get rid of this loophole here, page 3a, paragraph 2. We'll pay a token amount-one tenth of one percent, no more- and that will shield us from the P. R. and media attacks. We'll say we paid 'some' taxes."

The members of the board nodded. At this point, the board had become "yes" minions. They knew Jim wasn't feeling well and wanted to get the meeting over with.

"One more thing," Jim continued, commanding their full attention. "On the environmental case, did we get it out of Frisco or does that wacko activist judge still have her paws on it?"

The subsidiary's Corporate Counsel, attorney Black, responded from the other end of the table. "We are still trying to get the venue changed to L. A., sir. We have filed several petitions for that, but the Circuit Court keeps saying that Frisco has jurisdiction."

Jim frowned. "Well, these judges out here are elected officials, we'll get rid of her in the next election. Set aside a half million bucks to give to her opponent's Super PAC. We'll make that back twentyfold when we get rid of her."

With that, Jim concluded the meeting. Mike, to his left, again inquired about Jim's health. Jim's plan to catch Flight 957 was now under question. "You'd better take me to the hospital, Mike," Jim conceded.

V.

Flight 957 was taking off from San Francisco at noon Pacific Time on a July day. Karl, who had closed the big derivative deal the night before, was stuck in traffic with his mistress, Tracy. He was on his cell phone with his wife, Linda, who was back in New York. "I'm stuck in traffic, I missed the plane. I'll let you know about the later flight." Karl ended the call to Linda.

"I hate listening to you talk to her on the phone," Tracy bristled. "You're always trying to appease her. You have me, why don't you just get rid of her?"

Jim Drake's appendix was inflamed and could burst at any time. He needed surgery and, as doctors told him, "You're not going anywhere." Jim would not be on flight 957.

Laura placed her hand in her mother's as the flight began takeoff. Grace squeezed her daughter's little hand tightly. "It's O.K., honey, everything is O.K."

The deaf boy looked up at Maria as the flight took off. He crossed his arms in front of his heart like a shield, and then pointed to Maria. She smiled at him, and kissed him on the forehead.

VI.

"Has anything turned up yet? *Anything?*" Federal Aviation Administrator David Winton was on the phone with Sebastian Jones, the head of the FAA's Chicago branch. It was late August, more than a month after Flight 957 had left San Francisco.

"I know it's had to believe, David, but we just haven't found anything. Nothing has turned up. No wreckage, no bodies, nothing." Sebastian dreaded these calls, because he simply didn't have any answers. This had been going on since the day after the plane vanished. Would it ever end?

"Now you listen to me, Sebastian," David continued, not missing a beat. "I want to make sure I understand this. Fight 957 was cruising at thirty thousand feet and was detected on radar all the way from Frisco to about 30 miles west of Chicago. That much we know, right?"

Sebastian rolled his eyes. "That's correct, sir." They had already had this conversation on at least nine occasions.

"And then, it just disappeared off radar. No descent, no downward spiral. It was just traveling at thirty thousand feet and it disappeared at thirty thousand feet. Is that what you're telling me?"

Feeling like a broken record, Sebastian replied, "Yes, sir."

David continued without pausing. "And there was nothing on radar that collided with it?"

"That's correct, sir, nothing."

"And you've found nothing on the ground anywhere in or near Chicago, and nobody has reported finding anything that might be from a plane. No wreckage, no debris, nothing?"

"That's correct, sir. That's accurate."

Then there was a long pause. Sebastian had heard this long pause before. Finally, David spoke, "Well, here's the problem, Sebastian."

Here we go again, Sebastian bristled.

"The families of the passengers are looking for answers. The media is looking for answers. Even the President of the United States has asked me about it. I can't just tell them the plane was plucked out of midair and magically disappeared. You understand, right?"

Sebastian took a deep breath. "I've got as many people working on it as I have available. But we don't have the resources we used to have. As you know, our budget has been cut substantially..." Sebastian was interrupted at that point.

"Yeah, yeah, I understand. But the longer this goes on, the harder and harder it is to explain. God doesn't just reach down and grab a plane and its occupants out of midair and take them up to Heaven..."

Now it was Sebastian's turn to interrupt. "Oh, no? He doesn't? Look, I know you can't tell the media or the families or the President of the United States what you just said. I get it. I guess we'll have to keep that thought to ourselves."

California Girl

Rick entered the house after a long day at work and he was stressed. A mistake at work could mean death for someone else and a trip to Leavenworth for him. He took off his security badge and placed it on the dinner table. Pausing to look around him, Rick shook his head. This was a nice house, without question, but he wasn't used to it yet. It wasn't his style, as he had grown up in a log cabin in Maine. This was an "open air" contemporary in a wealthy suburb of Los Angeles, near the ocean. He hadn't had much say in the matter, as his employer – a defense contractor specializing in aerospace engineering projects- had rented the house and placed him there while on assignment at the local facility. Engineers got the best treatment, but "best" was subjective. He reminded himself it was only a one year assignment. Underneath, he knew this project could (and probably would) run into a second year or longer, but he was keeping that thought buried for the moment.

Rick watched the sunset over the Pacific, and then turned on the Lakers game. They were playing the Knicks, and for the first time in his life, he found himself rooting for a New York sports team. He missed the east, and he had only been on assignment for three months. He knew it would be a tough year or two ahead, as he sipped on a Sam Adams Boston Lager. He went to bed at halftime, exhausted.

Rick awoke at two a.m. to urinate. Whenever that happened overnight, he diagnosed himself with old man syndrome, even though he was only 31. After washing his hands, Rick hobbled toward the bedroom when he thought he heard a child's voice in the spare bedroom. Of course, this was nonsense, he figured. "I'm still half asleep," he thought to himself. The house was really too big for one person, and one could start hearing imaginary sounds after a while. He went back to bed.

Those half - conscious suppositions, however, did not help him when he awoke the next morning. Fortunately, it was a Saturday and he had the day off. He needed it. When he arrived at the kitchen table for breakfast, he found not one but two unexpected visitors. Moreover, they were making themselves quite at home. A little blond girl, perhaps three or four years of age, was eating toast as she sat at the table. A petite young woman, presumably the girl's mother, was tending to her, pouring her a glass of milk and so on.

Rick stood motionless and silent against the pillar of the doorway. "But I want jelly," the girl protested as the woman spread butter on to her toast.

"Mommy doesn't have time to go to the market, all we have is butter, now be a good girl and eat up," the woman replied.

For perhaps the first time in his relatively young life, the sight of an attractive woman had absolutely no effect on Rick. He was too taken aback by the circumstances to notice.

Rick was shell shocked. He could design the highest tech aircraft known to man, but this had him stumped. He looked behind him and looked around. He was trying to get a sense as to whether there were any other intruders in the house. His impression was that there were not, but who could say, at this point. Rick approached the woman, placing his hands on the back of an empty chair. "Excuse me, can I help you?" he began, one eyebrow raised. The woman not only ignored him, but appeared genuinely oblivious to his presence. She was biting her English muffin and looking at her daughter, as the girl looked down at the buttered toast with arms stubbornly folded and a scowl on her face.

"Hey!" Rich continued, louder. "Did you hear me? I said…" Rick stopped in mid-sentence. He had glimpsed the child from the corner of his eye and realized she was oblivious to his presence also, even as he raised his voice. It was one thing for a whack job adult to ignore him, it was quite another for a little girl to ignore a strange man yelling at her mother.

Rick looked back at the woman, who was still munching on the English muffin and looking at her daughter. Then he looked back at the girl, who was still staring down her buttered toast with her arms folded. Annoyed, Rick marched back into the bedroom. He hadn't even washed his face yet this morning and already things were going haywire. He scrambled the items on top of the bureau in search of his cell phone. Once he found it, he immediately hit the speed dial button to his liaison in the company's personnel department.

Jim Wright answered the phone at his home in Portsmouth, New Hampshire. He was used to the occasional complaint from an agitated engineer or two, including Rick. He knew who was calling because of Rick's distinct down east accent. "What the fawk is going on hea?" Jim heard.

"What's wrong, Rick?" Jim replied, confident he could diffuse whatever the issue was. Rick could, however, be a challenge. Jim once asked him about the high price tag of one of his expense reports, to which Rick replied, "Well I don't make the travel arrangements, so tawk to somebody who gives a fawk."

"What do you mean, 'What's wrong'? You've got some woman and her child living in this house. Who are they? What are they doing here? No one told me about this. How am I supposed to concentrate…"

"Whoa, wait a minute there, Rick, what are you talking about?" Jim asked, cutting in. This didn't sound right at all, Jim thought. He usually let a ticked off engineer vent for a while before offering a voice of reason, but not this time. What on earth was Rick talking about? A woman and a child living in the house? If so, it was just as much a mystery to him as it was to Rick.

"There's somebody here, in this house. She's down in the dining room right now eating breakfast with her daughter. Somebody better straighten this out..."

"Wait Rick, wait. You're saying that there is a woman and a child making themselves at home in that house. If so, they are squatting it. I didn't approve that and no one else would have either. Something is really wrong here, she must be crazy..." Jim opined, getting somewhat alarmed himself.

"Well, I figured that much, she's crazy all right..." Rick concurred.

"Don't confront her yourself, Rick. Don't take matters into your own hands. You need to call the police. The lady is trespassing; the police will come down and handle it. Call me back later and let me know how it goes," Jim advised.

"Fine, I'll call the police," Rick said before hanging up and doing just that. He had to spell out exactly what the problem was twice, from start to finish, as the incredulous dispatcher on the other end of the line tried to grasp what he was saying.

"All right, then, I'll send somebody out," the dispatcher concluded.

Rick stayed in the bedroom and looked out the window until the police car arrived, twelve minutes after he'd con-cluded the call to the dispatcher. He quickly left the bedroom, passing by the woman and her daughter as they looked at one of the girl's coloring books. Rick opened the front door and stepped outside, placing his hand on the cop's arm and closing the front door. "Look Officer, I got a problem," he began.

The cop looked Rick up and down. Rick suddenly realized he was still barefoot and in pajamas. "I know, the dispatcher told me about it on my way over here," the officer stated, his eyebrow raised as he continued to look Rick over. He removed Rick's hand from his arm. "Don't touch me again," he said, sternly.

"Right, sorry officer, but you've got to do something about this. She's just in here, right at the dinner table."

Both eyebrows ascended the officer's forehead at that point. Maybe, he reasoned, just maybe this wasn't a crackpot call after all. He put his hand on his gun. "You stay here, I'll go in…"

The officer entered with a measure of caution. He looked at the dinner table and saw no one. He then did a quick canvassing of the first floor and then reported to the dispatcher through the devise on his lapel. "There's nothing here, this guy's a whack job."

"That's what I thought," the dispatcher concurred.

The officer opened the front door. "They must have escaped out the back, there's no one here now. If you want to talk to somebody about this, a professional, I mean, that can be arranged."

"I don't want to talk to anybody about it; you're the person I want to talk to. They're here, I'm telling you," Rick ranted angrily. He stormed past the officer and into the house. He saw the petite woman standing by the dinner table, making eye contact with him and acknowledging his presence for the first time. Her face suggested she didn't understand what all the fuss and commotion was about. The young girl was sitting quietly at the dinner table, scribbling in her coloring book. She was well mannered and adorable. She did not look up at Rick or the officer.

"See? They're right *there*!" Rick adamantly declared as he looked at the officer. Rick saw that look on the officer's face again, with one skeptical eyebrow raised. Again, the officer saw no one.

"So there they are," chided the cop. He was a veteran of the force and had seen some strange things in his day. He was weighing his options. "Something tells me we're going to have a heck of a time trying to get them out of here," he continued.

Rick looked at him, perplexed. "What do you mean? They should be easy to remove. I'm sure you've removed tougher customers than this." The officer looked at Rick silently. Rick realized the officer didn't believe him. What was wrong with him? How could he have made it onto the police force if he couldn't see what was right in front of him?

"Look, they're right here," he continued, pointing again to the trespassers, but again drawing only a blank stare from the cop. Rick marched over to the woman and grabbed her by the arm. He could feel the real flesh and blood substance of her arm as he grabbed it and turned to show the officer. "See, she's right *here*: *RIGHT HERE*!!!"

As Rick's voice escalated and he continued grabbing at air, the cop decided the situation had to be defused. He was dealing with a delusional crazy person, or perhaps someone on an LSD trip. Either way, the cop had had enough. "I'm calling someone to help you out. *STAY* where you are, and don't move."

The sternness of the officer's voice made Rick realize that the officer truly was not seeing what he was seeing (even feeling, as his hand continued gripping the young lady's right bicep.) Somehow, something was terribly wrong here, Rick understood. Things just weren't as they seemed.

Rick quickly remembered the necessity of a security clearance for his job. If he was somehow found to be crazy, justified or not, he would lose his security clearance. If he lost his security clearance, he would lose his job. He knew he had to change his tune, and fast.

He let go of the woman's arm, and smiled at the officer. "I'm sorry officer, I can see now that this whole thing is just a misunderstanding. I sleep walk once in a long while and I guess I must have called you in my sleep. That's why I'm still in pajamas. I just snapped out of it now. There is no problem here, officer, sorry to have disturbed you."

Rick looked nervously at the officer, hoping he had fooled him. The officer appeared to be on the fence, not sure whether to take Rick into protective custody or not. After all, he *could* have been sleep walking, the cop supposed. "Well, if that's the case, I'll let you be so you can clean up and start your day. You sure you don't need any help?"

Whew, that was a close one, Rick thought. He felt he'd dodged a bullet there. "No really, I'm fine, but thanks so much."

Of course, Rick still had the same problem had he started with. There were still trespassers in the house, and they had to be dealt with somehow. Didn't they? How could they be dealt with if the police wouldn't get involved and if the woman wouldn't listen to him and barely acknowledged him?

Rick called Jim Wright back in New Hampshire and stated the police had come and removed the squatters. "It went smoothly without incident," he asserted. "It turned out not to be much of anything, I doubt there will be a need for any sort of report."

"Glad to hear it, let me know if you have any more problems," Jim replied as he poured food into his dog's bowl.

Rick continued trying to communicate with his "guest," but he continued to get no response whatsoever. "Who are you?"... "What is your name?"... "Why are you here?"... "You can't be here... you are trespassing... you have to leave...do you hear me?" All to no avail. He even resorted to trying to communicate with the child. "Is your mother deaf?"... "Can she hear?"... "Where is your dad?"... and so on. But the girl just ran to her mother and hugged her leg tightly whenever Rick tried to talk to her. Rick did notice a sad look on the girl's face when he asked about her father.

Rick noticed a plate of pasta had been set out for him at dinner that evening. The girl and her mother were already seated and smiled at him when he approached the table. Rick reluctantly sat in the chair as he looked at the mysterious but increasingly familiar woman. He started twirling spaghetti in his fork. He looked at the girl, who was cutely imbibing one long strand of spaghetti. As Rick leaned over and brought the fork to his mouth, he also noticed a Sam Adams Boston Lager had been set aside for him within easy reach.

Six days passed. Rick had become resigned to the situation and wasn't minding it as much as he had thought. When at home, he kept his wallet and his security badge in the wheel well inside the trunk of this car. The girls must have occasionally left the house when he was at work during the day as the refrigerator was always stocked. He didn't have to go food shopping anymore, and he never ran out of beer. He also didn't have to clean the place, as he noticed that was happening as well.

Aside from dinner time, Rick ignored his house mates during those six days. Well, at least he pretended to. A couple of times he found himself admiring the woman's figure. He would also get a kick out of some of the silly things the little girl would do and say. It became clear that neither of them were deaf or mute, they simply chose to ignore him, it seemed.

The following Friday night, he put on his best clothes, some cologne, and went to a dance club in Los Angeles. He was having a good time, meeting and flirting with lots of women. He was also drinking a little, a habit he was perhaps relying on a bit too much to relieve stress from work. As he stood against the bar in the crowded club at around 11:15, he was approached by a very attractive brunette whom he had conversed with off and on over the last couple of hours. She had a perfect figure and wore a blue mini dress with high heels. She was the type of girl that east coast boys fantasized about growing up when they thought of California. She looked right at him, with a big smile on her face.

"So, are you going to take me home and show me your place? I'd love to see it," she wondered aloud. Rick knew what she was saying.

"Sure," he began, but then stopped himself. "Oh, wait a minute. My place, it's kind of... uh, kind of a mess right now. I'm still moving stuff about..."

"No problem," she assured him. "We'll go to my place. My roommate's visiting her parents in San Diego this weekend, so I've got the place to myself." Her smile seemed to intensify.

Rick was quite aroused by the prospect of being with the gorgeous young lady. For obvious reasons, she had never had to ask a guy twice before. "That sounds..." but again Rick cut himself off in mid-sentence. There was a long pause. The young lady was perplexed. "You know what," Rick continued, "I'm going to have to pass. Right now just isn't a good time for me to be starting anything."

"Sure, I get it, not a good time," the young lady said, with a touch of sarcasm, before turning around and disappearing into the crowd.

The guests were in bed when Rick got back to the house, around 12:30 a.m. For the first time, he opened the door to the spare bedroom to check on them and make sure they were still there. Rick caught a glimpse of them as they slept, thanks to a nightlight the child liked to have on all night. He quietly closed the door and went to bed.

The next morning, a Saturday, he woke up late. The guests had already had breakfast and the child was working on her coloring book in the play room. Rick picked up a magazine and started reading it nearby. After a while, he looked over at the little girl. She seemed very content, as she colored with blue, purple and green crayons. He put down the magazine and sat down next to her. After watching her for a while, he started coloring some of the pages himself. "You did a real good job on that one," he said, smiling at her as he pointed to a dolphin she had colored blue.

"Thanks, I'm really good at this," she said, nodding. It was the first time she had spoken to him, and he was pleasantly surprised.

"What's your name," he asked, hopeful he might finally get an answer to a question he had for a full week.

"Amy," she replied, without looking up from the coloring book.

"Well, Amy. I'm Rick…" but he was interrupted there. "I already know your name is Rick," she said, as if he should have been aware of the fact.

"Well, anyway," Rick continued, "I have a question for you, Amy. It's something I have been wondering about. You are a smart girl, I bet you can tell me this. How come the police man couldn't see you or your mom when he came here? How is that possible?"

Amy looked at him with a confused look on her face. After about ten seconds, she finally responded. "No police man ever came here," she stated, matter of factly.

Rick was stunned at first, but then figured the young girl must be playing a game with him. "Of course a police man came here. He stood right in the doorway while you and your mom were at the dinner table. I put my hand on your mom's arm and started talking loudly to the police man. Surely you must remember that."

Again, all Amy could offer him was a blank stare, and a lengthy one at that. "No police man ever came here. If a police man had been here, I would have remembered that. It would have scared me," she stated resolutely. Then she looked down at the book and continued her coloring, having moved onto the giraffe on page 11.

Rick looked at the window in the wall behind the girl for some time, appearing to look "into space." He then resumed coloring, commenting on how nicely Amy could color along the way. At some point, he realized the girl's mother was standing right next to him, looking down at him and Amy as they colored. He looked up at her and saw her smiling, as the sunlight from the window made her blond hair seem to glow. She kneeled down next to him and planted an affectionate kiss on his left cheek. Then she quickly kissed him on the lips, mindful of her daughter's presence.

"I'm Vanessa," she advised, her faced beaming with a very broad smile as her eyes seemed to glisten in the light of the window. He gazed at her face. Somehow, at that moment, she resembled the sunrises he remembered from back east.

The Chosen

Marisa walked home from school, as usual, through Anderson Park. It was a quarter mile trek, harder in winter, but the temperature had climbed to a comfortable 48 degrees on this April afternoon. At sixteen, she was looking forward to getting her driver's license so she wouldn't have to walk every day. She'd have to spar with her older sister, Lisa, for access to the car. Even still, she'd get to drive it enough to make her lifer easier, she figured. As usual, her mother would have to be the mediator of these disputes, as her father lived several hours away.

She took note of the ducks as she passed by the pond, a sign that spring was on its way. The ice had disappeared as well, and she chose to pause on the bridge and gaze at the pond for a short while. The wind blew her curly blond hair behind her as her chin rested in the palm of her hand. She was in no hurry to go home, so she left the bridge slowly and with reluctance.

As she walked though a familiar wooded path, she noticed that something seemed out of place in the corner of her right eye. Immediately, she turned in that direction, thinking it might be a stray animal of some size. She then realized it was not animal, and it was not moving. It was just lying there.

Marisa rushed to get a closer look, then stopped in her tracks. *Is he homeless?* she wondered. *Is he sleeping?* The man appeared to be in his late thirties or early forties. Something told her, perhaps his utter stillness, that he was not sleeping. Something told her he was dead.

"Hello," she called out to him. No response. "Hello, are you alright?" she shouted, to no avail. She looked around, to see if there was anyone else was nearby. There was not, she was alone. She approached slowly, knelt beside him, and placed her fingers on his neck. Cold, and no pulse. She placed her fingers on his wrist. Cold and no pulse. She then took out her cell phone and called 911.

Four months passed. From time to time, she wondered about the deceased man she had found in the park. After the newspapers initially reported the story, however, she had heard nothing further. The papers had quoted a policeman as having said the man probably died "shortly before being discovered." It was early August now, and the high temperature on this day was expected to be in the eighties. In another month's time, Marisa would have her driver's license and would have started her senior year of high school. She was looking forward to it, as her summer had taken on a limbo like emptiness. To break up the monotony, she walked to the local convenience store in search of a magazine to read. She picked one up, along with a cola, and headed back home.

Boston in the summer. Better than Boston in the winter, but still not ideal. Eighty- five degrees would be fine if not for the humidity. But Boston could get humid, and today it did. She found this made it harder to breathe. Stopping at an intersection, she waited for traffic to stop before crossing the sidewalk. A Mercedes went by, then a Lexus. Status symbols, she noted. She then took note of a Boston police station on the other side of the crosswalk. Curious, she decided to stop in and find out what the police had learned about the deceased man. *What was his name?* she wondered. *How did he die? Was he married? Did he have children?* All she really knew of him was his face, which she remembered quite vividly. His face was slender, with a high forehead and prominent bone structure.

"Could I speak to Detective Peters?"

The middle -aged woman behind the plastic partition evaluated the teenage girl. *Beautiful, especially her hair. Pleasant demeanor. Could go far in life,* she thought.

"Why do you want to see Detective Peters?"

"Oh, he was the guy I talked to last April in Anderson Park. I mean, he was one of the officers who came to the park when I called 911."

"Why did you call 911?"

"Oh, I was the girl who found the body of a man who died there."

The woman looked at the girl silently for a few moments. "Have a seat, I'll call him."

Detective Peters' office was small and cramped with case files and other items like a coat rack and filing cabinet. She sat across from him as he sat behind his desk.

"How can I help you, young lady."

"Well, I came to find out more about the man I found in Anderson Park."

"Who?"

The detective's memory couldn't always keep every case straight. They all tended to mesh together after a while.

Marisa was somewhat taken aback. "In Anderson Park, back in April. I found a dead man just lying there. I called 911 and you and this other officer responded. I don't remember the other officer's name, though. You met me in the park and I showed you…"

"Oh, that's right, I remember now," he recalled. *What did ever happen with that case?* he wondered. "Here, let me look up that case on the computer."

He sifted through the cases from April. *There it is, deceased subject, Anderson Park.*

"What would you like to know?"

Marisa was surprised by his question. *Doesn't he know what I want to know?*

"Well, I was wondering who he was…like…what was his name?"

The detective looked at the computer screen and started moving his mouse around, sifting for information.

"We don't know," he replied.

Marisa's jaw dropped. She was stunned. "What do you mean you don't know? How can you not know? What are you talking about?"

The detective noticed that the young lady was getting very flustered and upset. He may have put an adult witness in his or her place at this point, but decided to go easy on the teenager.

"In a large city like this, it sometimes happens that a person has no identification on them at the time of their death. We ran his fingerprints, DNA profile and dental records through the NCIS database to see if it matched anyone in the country with a criminal history. It did not. There was no match. We put a page on our web site, with a description of the unidentified man, asking anyone with information to come forward, but no one…"

"So that's it? That's it? He's just nobody?"

"He's not nobody. We believe he may have been from somewhere else, I mean from another country. We usually would have been able to identify an American by now. We give unidentified people like him the name of John Doe, or if it's a female, Jane Doe…"

"John Doe and Jane Doe? You mean you have women like this too?"

Marisa seemed to be getting more upset by the moment, and the detective's patience was being tested.

"Well, Miss, what did you think we did in such cases? When someone had no identification and the fingerprints didn't match…"

"I don't know… I guess I just thought you…I don't know, that you held onto the body until you found out who it was…or something."

"Well, Miss, we certainly couldn't do that. The morgues are almost full as it is, with ongoing criminal inquiries and so forth. And some people never get identified. We can't hold onto their bodies forever."

She looked at him silently for five or six seconds. She was now leaning forward in her chair. "Well, where is his body now, then?"

"We had to bury him in a pauper's graveyard?"

"A what graveyard?"

"A pauper's graveyard. Every big city has them. It's a place where unidentified or unclaimed people get buried," he replied. He leaned forward in his chair and took a good look at the teenager. *What teenager comes to a station and asks all these questions? Doesn't she have a boyfriend or Instagram or Snapchat to keep her…*

"Well do you know why he died? I mean, what caused him to die?"

Detective Peters sat back in his chair and folded his arms onto his stomach. Thinking the matter over, he took a deep breath. "I suppose that's public record at this point," he finally said. Refocusing his attention on the computer screen, he again manipulated the mouse. He then downloaded the death certificate.

"The cause of death was a heart attack."

She looked down at the floor, shaking her head. "Didn't anybody call? Or file a missing person's report? Like a family member or friend or anything?"

She looked back up at the detective. He shook his head back and forth, silently.

"Where is this pauper's graveyard? Which plot is his?"

"I suppose that's public record, also," he answered, turning his attention to the computer once again.

"I need you to drive me somewhere," Marisa informed Lisa. Rolling her eyes, the older sibling lamented, "What kind of jaunt do you want to go on this time? I'm looking forward to when you get your license…"

"Me too, but I need you to take me somewhere and it can't wait until next month. It's nearby, it won't take long."

Rolling her eyes again, Lisa assented. "You better know exactly where this place is. I'm not getting lost and then just driving around."

As they got close to the destination, Marisa had no choice but to reveal the nature of their outing. "Look, I have my reasons, okay? The place we're going is called a pauper's graveyard."

"A what?" Lisa barked, bewildered.

"It's a pauper's graveyard. It's a place where they bury people when nobody claims the body or when they don't know who it was that died. It's the place where they buried the guy I found in the park. They never found out his name or anything."

The car was stopped at a red light. Lisa turned to her sister and provided her with a blank stare. "You're kidding me," she asserted. Marissa shook her head. "I wish I was kidding."

"Take a right here, it should be the third plot down on the right," Marisa informed her sister. Lisa obliged, still mystified as to why this outing was necessary, but willing to follow through with it now that she'd been informed of the circumstances.

The sisters stood in front of the marker, looking down at it. "John Doe, found in Anderson Park in Boston, April 8th, 2017."

Marisa looked up from the marker and around her. "There are quite a few John Does and Jane Does here," she observed, her voice tinged with sadness.

"I imagine so," Lisa gathered. "You said that's what a pupper's graveyard is, right?"

"Pauper's graveyard. It's a pauper's graveyard, not pupper's graveyard," Marisa stated, looking back down at the marker.

"It's wrong," Marisa continued. "It's wrong that they are all given the same name."

"What difference does it make. If nobody knows their real names…"

"It's wrong," Marisa repeated, her voice getting louder. "They should give them all different names. This guy, that I found, I remember how he looked. He didn't look like most people. You wouldn't have mistaken him in life for someone else. I could tell, he just looked like himself. Now he has the same name as all these other people, all these people who were different than he was. All these people who looked different, thought different, cared about different things, loved different people…"

"Look, I can't follow anything you're saying. You keep jumping from one subject to another. You're talking too fast. I'm going to go back to the car, I'll wait for you there. Don't take too long."

Lisa sat in the car, windows down, as a slight breeze softened the summer heat. She turned on her cell phone. She considered posting a selfie from the pauper's graveyard, but then thought it would be in bad taste. As she reviewed the most recent posts on her Instagram stream, she could hear a sort of whimpering from the direction of her sister. Lisa looked out of the passenger side window and noticed her sister was crying. Kneeling next to the flat marker on the ground, Marisa was leaning forward, placing both hands against the marker, her tears falling onto it. Lisa watched her sister for some time. *Leave her be, she's always been a little odd. She'll be alright. She'll come to the car soon.*

Lisa then turned from the passenger side window, and refocused her attention on Instagram.

Victoria's Dream

Victoria was asleep within minutes. At her age (all of nine years) it didn't take long. Once she was out, she was out for the night. Even a full blown riot just outside her window wouldn't rouse her. Such a riot was not likely in the quiet suburb of Watertown, Massachusetts where she lived her parents and her cat Jake, whom she was very close to.

Around midnight, some three hours after Victoria had gone to bed, she began to see colors, or something resembling colors. Deep blue, light blue, green, orange, red and yellowish images appeared before her. They seemed to take the form of a canvas, spread out like one of those tarps one would see covering a baseball field during a rain delay. The canvas was above her as she lay on the ground, fading from one color to the next and back again. Then it would take on all of the colors at once, each seeming to melt into the other, causing an almost kaleidoscope type visual. The canvas slowly waved in the wind, causing her to think briefly that she was under water, looking up at the surface. This went on for some time, like a large flag does on a mildly windy day.

Eventually, her position relative to the canvas of colors began to change. She felt herself being elevated into and through the canvas. She was surrounded on all sides by colors as wind blew her about as though she weighed no more than a feather.

The next thing she knew, she was sitting alone on a long beach. The day was overcast. Her knees were up toward her chest and her arms were wrapped around her knees. She was wearing a long, white dress. It was the only such dress she owned. As she watched the waves come in and crash on the shore, the wind cooled her face and blew her long hair back.

She rose slowly from her sitting position and walked toward the shore. For a moment, it seemed as though she was watching herself from a distance rather than inside herself as she walked. After a

short while, this sense faded as her bare feet started touching the water. She waded further in, seemingly in a trance. The waves crashed against her waist, her dress now soaked. Her body swayed from left to right but kept moving forward. A moment later, she was submerged. Darkness then surrounded her. As her descent continued, it got darker still, and a feeling of cold embraced her whole body.

A long time seemed to pass before a beam of light made it through the water's depth and landed on her face. As she looked up at it, the feeling of cold started to subside. She began a slow ascent as the beam seemed to pull her upward. The water changed as she got closer to the surface, becoming clearer and warmer. Finally, she broke the surface. The water was again waist deep, and her eyes widened as she looked around her. Large rocks to her left and right formed a cascade around a waterfall directly in front of her. A whirlpool at the bottom of the falls swirled over the lower half of her body. The day was sunny and beautiful. Tall pine trees above the rocks towered over her. The fall's water glistened brilliantly as it crashed into the whirlpool below, sending a mist slowly up towards the sky. She remained in this place, gazing at it, for some time.

Victoria's eyes opened at around 7:30 a. m., and she sat up in her bed. She ran her hands over her face and pulled her hair back behind her head. She then noticed Jake curled up at the end of her bed, near her feet. The cat was looking right at her, into her eyes. Victoria had a sense the feline had been watching her for some time. A moment later, Jake lost interest and jumped onto the carpeted floor.

Reflection

Ian arrived at the park at 6:30 a.m., a little later than most mornings. He was training for a 5K race and this park, at the edge of his small Vermont town, was the perfect proving ground because its trail was exactly three miles around. As always, he started near the entrance where three wooden benches stood side by side. He spent ten minutes stretching his five foot ten inch frame before starting off on his run. He usually would have taken fifteen minutes to stretch but he was behind schedule this morning. His first case at the local courthouse was scheduled for 8:30 a.m. The judge he was scheduled to appear before that day, Ian knew, did not take kindly to attorneys who showed up late for a hearing.

As he made his way around the park, he tried to erase the morning news from his mind. He had listened to the national news on the radio on his way to the park. One report was about the upcoming Obama-Romney election and the predictions various polls were making. Another report was about the unemployment rate. To Ian, the news seemed to simply repeat itself and he didn't understand why he bothered listening to it at all. He believed it was best if his mind was empty while he ran. In fact, the one time he had experienced the "runners high" was an occasion when his mind was completely empty of intrusive thoughts. It had been a couple of years earlier, while training for a marathon, when he had begun having feelings of invincibility around the sixteen mile mark. He felt as if his mind and body could literally keep going forever. It was a tremendous feeling he had not experienced before or since.

Making the final turn of this morning's run at about 6:55 a.m. he could see the three benches a little ways ahead. To his surprise, the park had another visitor. Sitting on one of the benches at this early hour was a young woman, perhaps in her mid-twenties. She had a small child with her in a stroller. The child appeared to be about a year old.

The benches were Ian's finish line. He would be done with his run and figured he would have time to go home, shower, grab a quick breakfast and still make it to the court-house on time. The woman noticed him coming, however, and her reaction to his presence stopped him dead in his tracks. She stood up from the bench and put her hands on her hips, looking right at him in anger. Ian didn't know who she was but she did look vaguely familiar to him.

"What the hell do you think you're doing?" she railed, seemingly loud enough to wake the occupants of the nearest house.

Ian was speechless for a moment or two. He looked the woman over, noting that she appeared to be roughly five and a half feet tall with blonde hair. She was wearing running gear herself.

"I *__beg__* your pardon?" he pleaded.

"You heard me" she retorted, her resolve entirely intact.

"Who are you?" Ian responded, summoning the lawyer inside of him.

"Never mind that, how could you leave your son sitting in a stroller, alone in the park, while you go off jogging? Don't you know he might have been kidnapped, or he might have been injured, or he might have needed you for some other reason? I was just about to call social services..."

"Whoa, hold on just a minute there lady!" he commanded, interrupting her. "I think you've mistaken me for someone else. Don't you know who the father of your own child is?"

At this, the woman seethed a deafening silence. Her eyes widened and Ian could almost see smoke emitting from her ears. Her fingers, still on her hips, began to tap against her as if she were playing an accordion.

"Now you listen to me, you S.O.B." she offered, taking two steps toward him and pointing at his face with her right index finger. Ian's eyes widened in turn, and both of his eyebrows went straight up. She's about to find out just how well I do listen, Ian thought to himself.

The woman continued, "I don't know who this boy's mother is, but I for one would have killed......"

"Wait a minute...wait a minute!!" he replied, talking over her. Now he was the one disturbing the neighbors sleep. "You mean to tell me that you're not this child's mother and you didn't bring him here this morning?"

The woman gave him a blank stare. She had heard his question to her, despite the heated back and forth. Her lips turned to the left side of her mouth and her head turned slightly to the right as she glared directly into his eyes and sized up his credibility.

The deafening silence returned, this time for about twenty seconds. The woman spoke in a quiet, but very serious tone. "You're not his dad?" she asked, her anger toward him deflated and replaced by an uncomfortable acknowledgment that there was a real problem here.

They both turned and looked at the child, who was sleeping quietly. Ian folded his arms as he looked down at the boy. The woman started massaging the back of her neck with her right hand. Then they both starting looking around for an adult, but there was no one in sight.

"When did you get there this morning?" he asked in a calm, non-accusatory voice.

"About ten minutes ago" she replied.

Ian looked at his watch. It was 6:59 a.m. "And the child was here, in this stroller, when you got here?"

"Yes he was, right here. There was no one else around. I'm sorry, but when I saw you coming this way, I naturally assumed…" Her reply was interrupted by loud cries from the stroller. The boy had awakened.

Both of them looked around, in all directions, for about thirty seconds, while the boy cried. No one was coming in response to the child's distress, it seemed. Ian and the woman looked at each other, making eye contact as the woman's lips again congregated on the side of her mouth. She turned toward the stroller, and lifted the youngster out and into her arms. She pressed the boy against her chest and whispered into his ear. "shhh…shhh….It's okay. Relax now, it's okay….."

Ian found himself checking the woman out from head to toe and realizing that had they met under more conventional circumstances, he may have asked her out. He liked blondes. She had a slender figure, and her smile (which he was just now witnessing for the first time as she tended to the boy) was quite attractive.

"I'm Marie," she stated as she turned her gaze toward him. The child had calmed down as he clung to Marie with both arms around her neck.

"And I would be Ian…..but some people call me S.O.B" he replied in jest, smiling at her. Marie laughed. Apparently she had a much softer edge than she had initially presented to him.

"I have a cell phone in the car, I'll go get it and call the police" Marie said, handing the child to Ian and walking away.

She knew the police would want to take a statement from both of them, so she waited for their arrival.

When the police arrived, at about 7:15 a.m., they spoke to Ian and Marie separately. When the officers finished their questioning, they formed a kind of huddle amongst themselves, excluding Ian and Marie from their conversation.

When the huddle broke, one officer approached Marie, and the other two Ian. "We are taking you both down to the station," they were told.

Ian was furious. He did not understand the need to be questioned at the station, as he had already told the police everything he knew and his statement was not going to change. He left a message for the court clerk explaining he would be absent from the hearing at 8:30 because he had witnessed a crime and was at the police station giving a statement.

The police put Ian in the interrogation room. The room housed only a table and chair. They had confiscated his cell phone before he entered the room.

Fifteen minutes passed. Finally the chief of police entered with two officers. The chief sat opposite Ian at the table, while the officers positioned themselves slightly behind him. One was to Ian's left, the other his right. Ian looked at the chief. "What is this? You know I'm an attorney, right? You know I'm admitted to the bar, don't you?"

"Oh, we're quite aware of your profession and standing in our small community sir. You needn't remind us again" the chief replied, his voice tinged with sarcasm.

Chief James Wrangle was bearded and in his early fifties. Small community or not, he had seen a lot in his day. He had a gruff, weathered look to him, which carried over to his demeanor. After what seemed like an eternity to Ian, the chief broke the silence and began his interrogation.

"Do you know, Ian, why we brought you into the station today?"

"Frankly, Chief, I don't. I told your officers everything that happened and everything I knew back at the park. You can ask that woman, Marie, she'll tell you the same thing I did. Someone left the child..."

"You see, that's just it" the chief said, interrupting, "that woman, as you called her, had an entirely different story about what happened than you did."

Ian looked at the chief with utter incredulity. After a lengthy silence, he replied "I beg your pardon, Chief Wrangle."

The chief looked briefly at the officer to Ian's left, then back at Ian. "In all my years on the force, sir, I have never heard of such wildly different versions of an incident as I heard this morning. You see, according to Miss Whitner."

"Who?" Ian asked, pleading ignorance. Chief Wrangle looked at him suspiciously for a moment. Upon concluding that the young man was genuinely at a loss, the chief elaborated.

"Marie. Remember? The other witness? Marie Whitner?"

"Okay, I didn't know what her last name was. Continue, please."

At that point, the chief made eye contact with the other officer, the one to Ian's right. "Miss Whitner states that she is your girlfriend, and she's been your girlfriend for the last four years. She states that you are the boy's father. She called us from the park this morning because, she said, you were delusional when you left the apartment this morning and even more delusional when she met you in the park to check on you. She wants us to take you into protective...."

"WHAT? WHAT DID YOU SAY?" Ian yelled. Chief Wrangle put both hands up in the officers direction, signaling them to stay put for the moment.

"I don't have a girlfriend and I don't have a child. This is the craziest thing I've ever heard," Ian continued, his voice only slightly reduced.

"Sir," the chief commanded before Ian could continue, "Did you tell the officers at the park that you are twenty eight years old?"

Ian was perplexed. He sat back in his chair and remained silent for about twenty seconds. His eyes revealed to the chief the state of bewilderment he was in. "Well," he replied, stuttering, "I don't remember specifically saying that to them, but I am twenty eight. So what? Did you miss my birthday and want to give me a present?"

The unflappable chief calmly responded to the interrogee's sarcasm with an order. "Let me see your driver's license."

Ian again sat back in his chair. His face was flushed red and perspiration was forming on his forehead. He was starting to realize that he may not have the upper hand. What on earth was happening?

"Sure, here it is."

The chief reached out and received the license with his left hand. He removed the license from its paper sheath.

"This says you were born in 1984, see?" Chief Wrangle said, now holding the license up to Ian's face.

"Of course it does" replied the attorney. "I told you, I'm twenty eight years old."

Chief Wrangle put the license on the table and placed his chin into his left hand. He looked at Ian silently, his face giving away nothing.

Ian, once again, appeared perplexed. "What? What is it?" he inquired of the chief.

Chief Wrangle removed his chin from his hand and sat back in his chair, placing his arms on the chairs arm rest. He looked at both officers, first toward Ian's left, then toward his right.

Ian took a deep breath as he observed the chief. "*This cannot be happening,*" he thought to himself. He leaned forward in his chair, giving the chief an icy stare. "What is today's date?" he inquired in a voice that seemed to almost threaten the chief.

"What is today's date?" Ian repeated, louder and leaning even more over the table.

"Today is June 26th."

"The **year**, Chief. I mean what year is it?" he urged in an increasingly menacing tone.

"It's 2014, son."

"TWO THOUSAND FOURTEEN!?!?" the interrogatee screamed as he stood up urgently, knocking his chair backward onto the floor.

The two officers grabbed Ian's arms.

"Let go of me!!" Ian screamed to no avail. "It's 2012. You people are crazy! Do you hear me? It's 2012 I said! Let me go!!!!"

"Wake up…..wake up….." Marie said as she shook Ian's arms. "For pity's sake, you're raising Cain inhere. You must have had a bad dream? Is that it? You had a nightmare?"

Ian looked up at his girlfriend of two years. She was blonde with a cute smile. "I don't know," he replied, "I don't remember any of it."

"Well, you need to get up. Your first case is at nine, you know how the judge hates it when you're late. Here, I'll turn on the radio. If you're not up in five minutes, I'm coming in to throw water on your face," she warned.

Ian rolled over on his side, still groggy. The radio was mumbling something about Obama and Romney campaigns and the most recent poll results with less than a month until the election.

Marie walked into the bathroom. The window was open and the October air sent a chill through her. Readying herself for work, she looked in the mirror at her hair. Her top and bottom lip moved to the left side of her mouth. *Hair's not perfect, but will do* she thought. She turned on the sink faucet and formed a cup with her hands. After splashing and drying her face, she checked herself in the mirror. *Face will do too, skip the makeup* she thought. She found herself looking into her own eyes for a moment. Then she looked down at the metal shelf attached to the bottom of the mirror. She picked up a thermometer- like instrument and held it up before her eyes. She realized that her at home pregnancy test had come back positive. Her eyes widened as her mouth opened in shock. Then she looked up at the mirror, into her own eyes again. She held eye contact with her herself, as though expecting her reflection to ease her mind with words of wisdom.

Just Before Midnight

It was too cold to wander the streets, so Ben spent the day inside Providence's Union Station. It was warm inside, there was a bathroom, and nobody bothered him there. He liked to hear the trains come and go. Occasionally, he toyed with the idea of hopping on a train to Connecticut or Boston as a stowaway and avoiding the ticket taker. He never actually brought himself to do so.

Voices threatened, taunted and humiliated him. He did not always know where they came from, but he was certain the people around him were out to get him. There was no doubt about that, he believed.

A young couple from New York exited the platform and entered the station. They walked by Ben with their two children, aged four and six. They were bundled up in winter clothes. The six year old, a boy, looked Ben in the eyes as he walked by and said something to his mother. Ben believed the child was speaking to him.

"They told me about you," Ben heard him say. "They told me who you are and what you've done."

Benjamin Clark had grown up in southern Massachusetts, near the Rhode Island border. He was an only child and his mother was an alcoholic. Academically, he was brilliant. He was a genius, in fact, doing college level mathematics as a freshman in high school. He never did drugs and never started drinking. He was a good kid, but he was always a little odd. People said he was "in a world of his own" and would grow out of it. He never did. Now 29 years old, both his parents had passed away and he had slipped through society's cracks. His father had tried to arrange it so that Ben wouldn't end up on the street, but he ended up there anyway.

"O.K., Ben, it's eleven o'clock." The officer on detail at the station was looking down at Ben. He was sizing up the vagrant's state of mind, and he had one hand on his taser gun, just in case. "They're closing up, you've got to get going. Do you have someplace to spend the night?"

Ben, unshaven and disheveled, nodded his head as if to say, "Yes." The officer knew he was lying, but decided not to fight that battle tonight. It is a free country, after all, he thought. "Well, you gotta get going now, Ben. I'll see you around."

Ben packed up his belongings, which included a sleeping bag, a duffle bag with clothes, and smaller bag with personal effects. One thing he did do relatively well was to keep himself clean and odorless. He washed up pretty good about twice a day at various locations around the city.

Ben headed into the streets of Providence, looking for a place to sleep. He noticed a couple of troublemakers, also homeless, in the park. So he decided against sleeping there. He considered one of the urban cemeteries where he sometimes slept, but decided that the closest one was too far to walk. He shivered as he made his way to Throop Alley. Throop Alley is literally an alley. It is a narrow walkway between two large buildings off South Main Street. It is not well lit, and the police usually don't bother Ben there.

II.

Helena had been having a great time at the night club. An exchange student from Norway, she'd gone out with two of her college friends on this Thursday night in December to party and dance. She was twenty one years old, about 5' 5" with blond hair and haunting hazel eyes. She was quite thin and had very pale skin. Her family's history in Scandinavia had been traced back to the Viking era, and although she spoke English well, her accent was somewhat thicker than that of most exchange students.

She'd been drinking since 8:30 and was very drunk. It was just before midnight and the club was very crowded. Helena and her friends had planned to stick together and to look after each other. Somehow, Helena had become separated from them and couldn't find them in the crowd. She was dressed provocatively in a short dress and high heels and was drawing the attention of some of the young men in the club. She danced with a guy from Brown, then a guy from RISD. She grinded him a little, something she wouldn't have done if sober. Somebody else pinched her behind as he walked by. At one point, all the lights in the club went down as the DJ began to announce the winner of some contest the club was having.

Disoriented, Helena decided that her friends must be outside somewhere, perhaps smoking. She noticed a side door nearby and walked over and pushed it open. For some reason, the alarm that that door was supposed to set off did not activate. Nobody noticed that she had left the club.

III.

Ben was taken aback by Helena's sudden appearance in the alley. He had just set up his sleeping bag and was about to lie down. The two stood motionless and looked at each other curiously for a good thirty seconds. She giggled. Ben understood that she was intoxicated. Helena seemed unaware of how cold it was given her skimpy attire. Ben was tempted to check out her body, to visually undress her in his mind. But he found himself somewhat mesmerized by her eyes and her face. He was struck by her facial features for some time. She lost her balance and lunged forward into his arms. He prevented her fall and then continued holding her in his arms as she gig-gled some more. Ben did not consider taking advantage of her sexually, but he did love having her in his arms. He weighed his options as she initiated a slow dance with him. Her arms were around his neck and her head was on his chest. Part of him wanted to keep it just like this somehow, but he knew there was a limit to how long it would go on. He seriously considered laying her down in the sleeping back and getting in with her. He wanted to hold her in his arms, keeping her warm and vice versa, for however long he could get away with it. But Ben happened to be lucid enough at this moment to understand that this was problematic. He wasn't sure how old she was, first of all. Twenty one? Maybe. Seventeen? Maybe. It had better not be the latter, he thought. Her friends, boyfriend, or somebody would come looking for her soon enough, and that could be trouble. What if she woke up sober in an hour or two and accused him of sexual assault? He was already on probation for a fight he got into with a man at the bus terminal about seven months earlier. He weighed these concerns against the desire to relieve, at least for a short time, the loneliness that had engulfed his existence for the last several years.

She swayed back and forth in his arms. After a while longer, she pulled away slowly. She looked into his face closely, as if she was trying to recognize him, but couldn't. "Thanks for the dance," she began. Ben barely understood her through the ac-cent and slurred speech. "I gotta go find Michelle and my other friend, Jane… I mean, Jen. Yeah, Jen. That's her name." Helena tried to open the side door from the outside, but it was locked.

"You better go to the front door. Just go that way and to the left when you get to the sidewalk," Ben said, pointing towards South Main Street.

"Oh, thanks sweetheart," Helena said before kissing him on the cheek. Ben watched as she left the alley, turned left on the sidewalk, and disappeared from his sight. "She'll find her friends and be O. K.," he thought. Somehow, he was already missing her. He got into his sleeping bag and was asleep within ten minutes.

IV.

Ben was biding his time in the train station again. It was January now, and it was even colder than it had been in mid-December. It was a Saturday and the station was busy. Ben could hear the announcement over the speaker. "Benjamin Clark is a horrible person who must be quarantined. If you see him, do not take matters into your own hands. Call the authorities immediately. Anyway, Amtrak train number 69 bound for Washington D. C. is now boarding on track five."

Ben looked to his right and noticed a local newspaper next to him on the bench. He picked it up and began to read the front page. There was an article about the President of the U. S. giving some sort of speech. Ben's eyes traveled to the bottom of the page where an article caught his eye. "*BODY IN PAWTUCKET CREEK ID'D AS MISSING EXCHANGE STUDENT FROM EUROPE,*" read the headline. Ben's eyes widened. The article continued:

> *A body found floating in a creek in Pawtucket has been positively identified as that of a missing twenty one year old college student from Norway. Helena Ramses was*

named as the deceased by the state coroner's office yesterday. Ms. Ramses disappeared from the Extreme Nightclub on South Main Street on the evening of December 16th. A friend reported her missing the following afternoon after being unable to locate her at the club and not receiving a call or text from her the next morning. Surveillance footage from a building across the street showed Helena, apparently intoxicated, approaching the club's entrance from the sidewalk near Throop Alley at 11:58 p. m. The club has two front doors, but Helena only tried to open the door to her left. When it wouldn't open, she appeared confused and then continued walking southbound on the sidewalk towards Steeple Street. After that, she was outside of the camera's view. An eye witness told police that she saw a young woman meeting Helena's description talking to two men on the corner of Water Street and South Main Street shortly after midnight. The young woman then entered a large, black S. U.V. that had been idling on the other side of Water Street. The witness said that it did not appear that she was forced into the vehicle. Police believe she either went voluntarily or was threatened into the vehicle. The S. U. V. immediately sped off as soon as the woman was inside. The witness stated that she was disturbed by the vehicle's hurried exit from the scene. She could not provide police with a license plate number. The coroner's office stated that Helena had been sexually assaulted and strangled. Authorities have notified her relatives in Norway...

V.

Ben put the newspaper down. He was breathing heavily and had begun to perspire. He started shivering. After a while, he settled down. He looked around the station at the travelers.

Many were businessmen with brief cases. There was a young woman with a suit case and a back pack. Ben threw his duffle bag over his shoulder and picked up his other bags. He exited the station into the frigid January afternoon air. He walked across the State House lawn, turned right and continued until he reached Orms Street. To his right, he could see the Marriott Hotel. A gust of wind chilled him to the bone. He crossed the street and began descending an exit ramp off Interstate 95. Ben sat down on the grass area between the ramp and the highway. Litter and debris covered the area. He placed his bags down beside him and crunched his knees up near his chin. He folded his arms and placed them on his knees. Turning to his right, he could see the oncoming, south bound traffic. The cars were moving at a steady clip of about 70 miles per hour. In the distance, Ben spotted a tractor trailer truck. He stood up, focused on the big rig. A car passed by. He walked onto the highway, turned and faced north. An ear shattering horn blared from the truck as it barreled forward. Ben lifted up his hands, and embraced the rig's front grill.

Leaving Karachi

Elise was not looking forward to her next "assignment." He did not give his name, saying only that he was from Karachi but had lived in London for nine years. "Why are you back?" she wondered. "Well, I'm here for a while now, my dad's not doing well. I used to come here, to this place, before I went to England. I'm not the kind of guy who, you know, makes much headway with the ladies."

She had figured as much. He was average looking, and quite awkward. He had no swagger. She could see he wasn't what women wanted.

"Is this what you do in London, also?"

"Yes, this is kind of how it is for me."

He had used his "nerd pass" -computer expertise, to escape a hardscrabble life in Pakistan and emigrate to the U. K. He now dual citizenship.

"Well, this isn't London," she replied, her voice adopting a cautionary tone. "And Karachi has changed since you left. I hope you know what part of town you're in. I hope you don't get lost down here. The police won't come to this part of Karachi. The *military* won't come to this part of Karachi."

His name was Adnan and he was thirty two years old. When he first started visiting brothels, about twelve years prior, he was surprised at the typed of conversations the young women would engage him in. In fact, he was surprised they wanted to converse with him at all. They did, and it was real conversation. There was no surface baloney. He quickly realized these women had difficult histories which had led them to their current circumstances. He didn't know the details, but he knew their histories had been painful. None of them were in a brothel because a sister had stolen jewelry and refused to return it. He knew there was a lot more to it, and maybe that's why he kept coming back.

He sat on the bed and looked up at her. She slowly removed her robe, unveiling herself to him. She had to play along, no matter how skeptical she was about the encounter. At the age of twenty five, she felt her beauty and sex appeal may indeed justify the attention and compliments she frequently received from her visitors. As Adnan lavished more of the same towards her, she smiled and performed a slow, 360 degree turn around for him.

He stood up and pulled her closer. She realized he was going to kiss her first, perhaps even make out with her first. This was uncommon, but not unheard of in her experience. Generally, she didn't like this part, but it was better than what was to follow.

He ran his hands through her hair, then kissed her gently and passionately for some time. His hands respectfully and considerately caressed her body as he continued kissing her.

She found herself enjoying the encounter much more than she had expected she would. She placed two fingers on his chin, interrupting a kiss. She found herself looking into his face. He was more handsome, and less awkward, than she had thought. "You're sweet," she opined, smiling at him.

Eventually he made love to her, an experience which lasted longer and pleased her more than she had expected.

Only one customer of the many in her mental rolodex could claim to have equaled him. He was a tall, young lawyer from Karachi who had visited her about two prior. She hadn't seen him since.

As Adnan was cleaning up, he griped, "Oh, damn."

"What, what is it?"

"Well, the condom broke."

This didn't concern her as much as it did him. "Don't worry about that, it's happened before," she advised.

"I suppose it has," he acknowledged.

"When are you going back to England?"

Her arms were folded as she sat up against the bed's headboard and watched him get dressed. She noticed a large, round birth mark in his upper right chest area.

"I'm not sure, it depends on how things go with my dad."

"I hope your dad gets better. Listen, I want you to visit me again."

"I might, we'll see..."

"And not just for the money," she inserted, interrupting him.

He stopped what he was doing and looked at her. They held eye contact silently for four or five seconds. "Come here," he instructed her. She approached him and they embraced. Their hug lasted about twenty seconds before he started letting go. She let go of him as well, but did not step back when the embrace ended. She just stood there, looking at him from a foot or two away. After another ten or twelve seconds, he began to speak when she suddenly pulled him back into another embrace. He swallowed whatever words he had intended to say to her. This hug was closer and lasted longer than the previous one. her arms were wrapped tightly around his shoulders and neck while her face was buried in his chest. He didn't dare pull away this time, keeping her in his arms until and unless she ended the hug. After a while, she slowly began to loosen her hold on him.

Later that evening, after four more customers had come and gone, she noticed a white plastic card on the floor. She picked it up and recognized the man in the photograph in the upper left corner of the card. It was Adnan. He had dropped a security card issued by his employer, a computer security firm in London.

Three months passed, and Elise's difficult life continued uneventfully. She slept during the morning, did some chores, and read newspapers in the afternoon. She had sex with men throughout the night. Adnan has not visited her since that night she met him. She had hoped he would return (to retrieve his security card, if for no other reason) but he had not. She still had the card among her personal possessions. It was her only link to one of the few special memories she'd had in her adult life.

One afternoon, while reading the newspaper in the "employee's lounge", Elise and two of her co- workers were approached by the brothel's owner. He was short, overweight and in his fifties.

"Get your things and go," he abruptly decreed. The ladies were stunned and looked at him silently. "The Taliban gave me an ultimatum. They told me to shut the place down or they would shut it down - their way. None of us want that."

The three women looked at each other in disbelief. Finally, Elise turned to the owner. "Where will we go? I have no place to go."

"Let's be clear about one thing. Where any of you go or end up is not my responsibility or my problem. That said, I will give you the names and addresses of a couple of shelters for women nearby."

"I didn't know there were shelters for women in this part of Karachi," Elise responded, raising one eye brow.

"Most people didn't know there were brothels here either," he replied.

The shelter's accommodations were a little better than the brothel's, but not much. At least there wasn't a parade of men marching in and expecting sex. Elise was given no specific time table for how long she could stay, but it was made clear to her that she could not stay indefinitely.

Shelter, however, was not foremost in her mind in the days following her departure from the brothel. Sickness was. Throughout the day, she experienced spells of nausea. Intense, relentless nausea. She wondered what was wrong? Did she have food poisening? Did she drink unsafe water?

One night, the nausea awakened her in the middle of the night. She drifted in and out of sleep for some time. The moon slightly illuminated the room as she lay quietly in bed. At around three thirty a. m., her eyes opened widely. She was no longer half asleep. She suddenly realized what was happening to her, and it was neither food poisening nor a water borne illness.

Being unwed and pregnant in some parts of the world is not a happy set of circumstances. In 2002, a woman named Safran Bibi in Kohat, Pakistan was sentenced to death by stoning for having a child out of wedlock. Her defense at trial was that her pregnancy had been the result of a rape, and that she could not have prevented it. Her defense was set aside by the magistrate presiding over her case. It was not that the magistrate did not believe her claims. He made no ruling on whether the incident was consensual or forced. He didn't have to, as it was irrelevant under the law. (-The New York Times, May 17, 2002, "In Pakistan, Rape Victims are Criminals", reported by Seth Mydans.)

Not knowing who to turn to or who she could trust, Elise was now in a state of panic. Her pregnancy had not started to show yet, but she knew it wouldn't be long. She knew she had to come up with some sort of plan - fast.

For the next few days, she was in a sort of mental fog and didn't leave the shelter at all. She spent her time between hoping that an answer would come to her and brainstorming to come up with one. One afternoon, while watching the news on television, a story was broadcast entitled "Karachi's Benazir." It was about a Cambridge educated human rights attorney who had returned to Pakistan to advocate for women's rights. She was doing so, the program pointed out, at risk of her own life.

"May I help you?" the woman behind the counter inquired of the young, tepid woman before her.

"I have a big problem. I need to see Mrs. Nasret Kol," Elise responded.

Attorney Kol's office was sparse. A tall, slender woman of thirty five, her demeanor could shift from gentle and inviting to sharp and cutting, depending on the situation. As she listened to Elise's story, she found her credible, and felt great sympathy welling up inside her. At some point, she stopped listening to Elise, and just watched her as she was speaking. She noticed that the young woman's mannerisms were tepid, innocent, and perhaps naive. The attorney thought she was cute, but also resilient and admirable. Hers was the story of a survivor, it seemed.

"This is why I'm here," Nasret thought to herself as she continued watching Elise. "This is why I came back to Pakistan."

Nasret arranged for Elise to stay in a safe house in the countryside outside of the city. For the birth, she arranged for a midwife whose services she'd employed previously and could be trusted to be discreet and confidential. An elderly woman owned the safe house and secretly hosted "troubled" young women in exchange for the assistance she needed at her advanced age. Elise cooked, cleaned, and provided care giving services to the kind old woman.

During the six months she spent in the countryside, Elise found that her stress and anxiety had reduced greatly, and her view of the world had changed. She realized there was more to life that tall buildings, smog, traffic, and people in a hurry. She had never experienced fresh air until she began staying with the old woman in the countryside. In many ways, those six months were the happiest of her life. The dilemma she was faced with, however, was never totally out of mind. It was always there, like a stranger watching her. Attorney Kol had laid out the reality of the situation quite starkly: unless some sort of path to asylum or citizenship in Europe could be found for her, a secret adoption to a childless couple in Karachi would be her only option. Failure to achieve one of those two outcomes, the attorney warned, could put her freedom -indeed, her very life- in jeopardy. Nasret promised to work diligently to find a legal way to get Elise to Europe and keep her there, and to notify her immediately if a path were found. She warned, however, that it would not be easy.

As the estimated due date approached, Elise was saddened, but not surprised, that no solution aside from the secret adoption had been found. Nasret had visited the week before, upset in her own right, and informed her that extensive legal research efforts had, "failed to yield a safe path for you to keep your child." The best she could offer, her voice cracking, "Is that I have submitted a proposal to change the law to all of Karachi's members of Parliment, but the bill just hasn't moved at all. I didn't tell them about you, of course, I just spoke in general terms about the need to change the law. Despite my pleadings, it has stalled, and even if it does eventually pass, it will be too late for you."

After a deep breath, Elise responded with gratitude. "I understand. You told me it would be a long shot. Thank you for your efforts and for setting me up in this house."

Before Nasret left, she had one more piece of information for the heartbroken young woman. "You may be interested to know this. The building you used to live in was burned to the ground by the Taliban."

"I don't understand, it was no longer a brothel. My captors had vacated the place."

"I know. The Taliban burned it down anyway."

A childless couple from the city were to arrive on the estimated due date. Three days sooner, however, Elise started going into labor early. The mid wife was called around 9:15 a.m. The old woman attempted to notify the adoptive couple as well, but she'd been unable to reach them.

Six hours of unspeakable pain. Elise had never experienced anything like it and hoped to never experience it again. Blinding, mind blowing, "what the hell just happened" type of pain. When it was finally over, the midwife (a short, heavy set woman of forty two from a nearby town) handed her a seven pound baby boy. As she pulled the child closer to her, Elise felt a connection which seemed infinitely stronger than anything she'd felt to anyone before. As the child's head rested against her chest, she felt strangely equal to every other woman in the world. It was as if she had somehow returned to the starting line of life's race and the punches life had dealt her never happened. Or, if they had happened, they no longer mattered.

She looked at the old woman and then at the mid wife. Smiling, she said, "Thank you both very much. Could I be alone with him for a little while?"

"Of course," the old woman replied. The two women left the room and walked outside to a courtyard adjacent to the house.

It was a cool, overcast fall day as the two ladies strolled through the courtyard. A mini maze wound its way around wooden partitions covered in vines. "You know what is happening here, right?" the old woman confided in the midwife.

"Yes, I've been doing this for a while, I know how this will play out. Where is the couple, anyway? They're usually at the delivery ready to scoop the child up before the biological mother gets any contrary ideas in her head."

"I tried to reach them, but they don't seem to be answering their cell phone. Maybe it is out of range or something. You know how those cell phones are."

The mid wife paused for a moment and looked around at the walled - in courtyard. Earlier, she had seen the surrounding landscape, with it's beautiful hills and streams.

"As far as safe houses go, this is a very nice one," she remarked.

"Yes, I imagine so," the old woman concurred. "My late husband did quite well in life. I kind of lucked..." Just then, a loud and urgent voice was heard from the open window on the second floor, directly above the women. "CALL NASRET!!! CALL NASRET!!! HIS FATHER IS BRITISH...I CAN PROVE IT, I CAN PROVE IT!!!"

"I can't require one of our citizens to take a genetic test merely because your client alleges a similar birth mark on the child's chest," opined the U. K.'s Consulate Inspector in Karachi, as he sat accross from Attorney Kol, his arms resting on his chest. "How do I know these people ever even met?"

He was in his fifties and had seen no shortage of false claims upon British citizenship in his day. He intended to retire and return the U. K. within a year.

Nasret Kol leaned forward in her chair, holding up a security card with Adnan's name, photo, and other identifying information. "He left this behind, and she picked it up and kept it," she advised.

The inspector put his glasses on and leaned forward. He recognized the employer as a computer firm in London he was familiar with. He took a good look at Adnad's name, photo, and job title on the card. It appeared legitimate to him. Then he turned his attention back to the attorney, and noticed that her jaw was clenched and her eyes were piercing into his.

Elise had never been on a plane before. She was a little scared to get on a plane with the baby, but her excitement over moving to London cancelled out whatever fears she had. After secretly conducted genetic testing had proved Adnan was the father, the British Consulate had come up with a cover story to the effect that she had married a British citizen prior to becoming pregnant, and was now emigrating to join him in London. Whether the Pakistani authorities truly bought the story or played along with a wink and a nod was unclear, but either way she was on her way to a new life. In fact, Adnan had agreed to take her and the child in upon their arrival, saying he wanted to "see how things go."

The baby started getting restless as the plane flew over Paris at midnight. It was a long flight for him, and he wasn't used to having so many people around as he slept. Elise took him into her arms and held him against her chest to put him at ease. After she quieted him, she looked out the window and looked down. She saw lights - thousands of them, as far as the eye could see.

Inside The Bubble

I. CLOSE CALL

A man had pulled over when he saw the wreck, and ran right to Wendy.

"I was the only one in the car," she advised. She was still gazing at the wreck, and had yet to visually acknowledge him. He was very surprised by her statement.

"You were in that car?" he marveled.

"Yes, I told you. I was driving it," Wendy asserted.

He looked at the wreck, and then back at her. "Miss, that car flipped over. The roof is damaged. How could you have come out of that uninjured? Are you sure you're alright?"

She ignored him, continuing to gaze at the wreck as if she were in a trance.

Unconvinced that she was even in the car, he walked over to it to get a closer look inside. As best he could tell, there was no one in the car, nor was there anyone else in the surrounding area. He dialed 911 on his cell phone.

"911, what's your emergency?"

"We've got a rollover here on County Road at the inter-section of…what is it…Birch Street."

"Was anyone injured in the accident, sir?"

"Well, that's hard to say. It appears the driver, a woman, was the only person in the car. But she wasn't in the car when I got here. She was standing near it, looking at it. She seemed more like a bystander than someone involved in the accident. She may be in shock. Someone better take a look at her."

II.   PLEA FOR HELP

"You are the best person to get to the bottom of it. You are a friend and a psychologist. Please, this is real and it is strange. I'm not the only one who's noticed it," Craig pleaded.

"So, let me see if I understand this again. Once every three or four months this happens, and it lasts for how long?" Denise was still scratching her head.

"It's usually three or four days. Sometimes five."

"Alright, and you're certain it's not once per month…"

"No, Denise, it's not her menstrual cycle or whatever. It's more than that. Something is going on with her," he replied, interrupting her.

Denise looked at him silently for a few seconds, her eye brow raised.

"Fine, and how would you best describe these four or five days?"

"She's distant, Denise. Very, very distant. Her personality disappears, her sense of humor disappears. It's almost like she's in a trance."

"Fair enough, Craig. I'll get together with her for lunch. I'll make it seem like we're just catching up on things, but I'll get her talking. And how long did you say this has been going on?"

"Ever since I've known her, since before we were married. I've known her for ten years, so it's been at least that long," he replied, shaking his head slowly.

III.   LUNCH IN NEW YORK

"I'm so glad we could get together," Denise began, casually looking over the menu.

Wendy weighed the menu options. Nice place, she thought. Denise had said lunch would be on her, so Wendy was impressed with her generosity. She was hoping to find something simple on the menu, so as not to run up the tab. "I know, it's been a while since we saw each other. I was so glad when I saw your e-mail, Denise."

The two women, both thirty-five years old, reminisced about old times at college. Denise pretended to open up with highly personal details of her marriage and her life. A formally dressed waiter poured water for them. Denise would end up spending about seventy dollars on lunch, not unusual for Upper East Side restaurants. Maybe Craig would reimburse her, maybe he wouldn't. No matter, she thought.

"And what about you, Wendy? Tell me about your life. How are things?"

"Oh, things are fine. Craig is great, and the kids are as well," Wendy answered, twirling spaghetti with her fork.

"I'm glad to hear it," Denise offered, looking at her companion closely. "But how about you? You can be honest with me. I know no one has it perfect… and trust me, I've heard it all. If you only knew of some of the things I've heard in my practice…"

Wendy's fork stopped twirling. Denise noticed her adam's apple rise and fall in her throat. "This is it," Denise thought to herself. "Here it comes."

"You've heard everything?" Wendy's tone was more rhetorical than inquisitive. It was as if she were about to add, "Well, you haven't heard this…"

"Just about everything," the psychologist claimed, reassuringly.

Wendy was now looking down at her plate. Her hand slowly resumed twirling the spaghetti. Finally, she looked up at Denise. "Well there is this one thing that happens, which I could tell you about, if you promise to keep it between us."

"Absolutely," Denise responded unequivocally. The wheels in her head were already turning as to how she would parse (but not "tell") Craig whatever she was about to hear.

Wendy let go of her fork, and clasped her fingers as both of her elbows rested on the table. "Well, Denise, here's the thing. Every so often, I go into this… this sort of… funk. It's hard to describe."

"Well, that's not unusual, you know. It's quite comm…"

"No, this is different."

Denise sat back in her chair and folded her arms over her stomach.

"Alright. Tell me about it."

"Every so often, I go through this phase when I feel very sorrowful for someone else. Someone I've never met. I can't relate to those around me, when this happens. It's like I lose three or four days of my life."

Denise leaned forward in her chair and sipped her water, keeping her eyes on Wendy the whole time. This did have her stumped, and she hadn't heard this one before. After a short time, she responded in the only way she could think to. "Who is this person?"

"That's the thing," Wendy explained. Her chest was rising and falling noticeably as her breathing got heavier. "I don't know her name. In fact, I only know one thing about her. I knowthat she died."

Denise had been a professional psychologist for seven years. Very rarely was she at a complete loss to understand a patient's symptoms. This discussion with her old friend, however, was one such occasion. She knew Wendy was entirely genuine and sincere. She knew Wendy believed what she was saying: that she was periodically grieving for a deceased soul she had never crossed paths with.

"Whenever you're ready," the waiter said, leaving the check for Denise.

"Do you know why this doesn't happen more frequently?"

"Not really, no. You see, most of the time, this doesn't happen. Most of the time, I'm fine and I have positive feelings for this person – a feeling of knowing that she is at peace. Other times, I'm not feeling anything for her, I'm just myself. It only happens once every few months, and it only lasts a few days."

Wendy gave her old friend a long look. "Let me ask you, Denise," she continued, somewhat assertively. Her chin now rested on the knuckles of her clasped hands while her elbows rested on the table. "What drew you to me? Why did you pursue a friendship with me at Columbia as intently as you did?"

Denise shifted in her chair, and took a deep breath. "You were, and still are, fascinating. Not everyone was drawn to you, some kids thought you were weird. But I was drawn to you. You had this, sort of…"

Denise was struggling to articulate her thoughts. She uncrossed and re-crossed her legs. "I always felt that I would be safe when I was with you. That we would be safe, even in this huge city. You seemed to have this…I don't know…protective bubble around you."

The two women looked at each other silently for four or five seconds.

"It's funny you should say that, because Craig says it too. He says I'm the luckiest person in the world. He often mentions the time I survived a plane crash, even though it wasn't really a crash. It was an emergency landing in a lake in Minnesota. Did I ever tell you about it?"

Denise's eyes widened as she shook her head, pleading ignorance.

"I was a little reluctant to get into the small plane in the first place. I don't like small planes. I was visiting a friend out there and we were on one of scenic rides over the forest. Before we could get up high enough, though, the pilot said that something was wrong. He said the engine was going to fail and he had to do an emergency landing. What he didn't tell us until afterwards was that there was no place to land. At the time, he said he had everything under control, but I could see he was very shook up. He ended up landing it in a small lake in the woods. Luckily, some people were fishing in canoes and came to us and took us each to shore."

"When did this happen?"

"Oh, this was about eight or nine years ago. Like I say, Craig seems to think about it more than I do."

"Well, this is the first I've heard of it," Denise acknowledged. "Of course, I do remember the car crash you survived, and that was a crash."

"Yes, then there was that," Wendy recalled. "The guy who called the cops, when he saw the wreck, said he had no idea how anyone could come out of it unscathed, and the policeman said that, too. I wasn't even injured, just scraped up a bit. Thank God I was alone in that car. Craig talks about that sometimes, too."

"Maybe we're onto something. Maybe you do have a guardian angel, someone who protects you during close calls" Denise observed, smiling.

Wendy laughed.

A few moments later, the smile departed Denise's face. She leaned forward, over the table.

"Wendy, if you ever need to discuss these phases you go through, when you are grieving the deceased person, you can talk to me about it in a professional context. Your insurance will cover it, and I will waive the copay for you. Just call my office and we'll set it up."

Wendy looked back at her friend. As she did so, she started rubbing her fingers over her chin repeatedly.

"How did your lunch go?" Craig inquired innocently.

"It went well, it was good to see Denise again." She did not elaborate.

"Remember, we're going to a cookout at my parent's house on Sunday," she offered, figuring he'd probably forgotten.

IV.   THE COOKOUT

Wendy's parents lived in Connecticut, about an hour's drive from New York City. Craig had nothing against her parents, but he didn't like making the trip to their house. If he could have his way, he'd never leave the city. Their two daughters, aged seven and four, were quiet in the back seat as the Volvo pulled into the driveway. Wendy's mother, Elaine, waived at them from the bay window of the house.

Hot dogs, hamburgers, corn on the cob. Fair enough, Craig thought as he kept an eye on his daughters while they played with a frisbee. "How's Wendy doing, how's she been?" Elaine wondered as she sat next to him. Craig didn't answer, he kept watching the children. "Has she gone through any more of those... you know... those spells?"

Craig reluctantly addressed the question. "She gets them occasionally," he answered, still watching the children.

"She used to get them when she was a child, too," Elaine recalled. "She always got them from time to time."

This got Craig's attention. He had always assumed it was an adult onset issue. He looked over at Elaine suspiciously.

"Step inside here," Wendy's father, David, requested of her. He sat behind his desk in the study. Books lined the wall behind him.

"Yes, Dad, what's this about," she inquired as she sat in a chair opposite him.

"Well, as you know, your mother and I are in our early seventies now. There is never a good time to talk about certain things, but at some point they must be discussed."

He pulled out a diagram of the family's cemetery plot from a drawer in the desk. "I want you to look at this."

She glanced down at the diagram, quickly realizing what it was. Then she looked up at her father.

"There are ten plots," he advised. With a pencil, he started pointing them out. "My mother is in plot one, my father in plot two." He paused without looking up. After a few seconds, he continued. "Uncle Jim is buried here, in plot three. Aunt Laura and her husband will go in plots four and five, when their time comes."

He looked at his daughter before taking a sip of water. "Here are plots six and seven. I want you to make certain, Wendy, that your mother goes in plot six, and that I go in plot seven. You may be running this show if one of us has alzheimer's or something when the other one dies."

He then paused and sat back in his chair, taking another sip of water.

"Okay, I get it," Wendy reluctantly stated. Her reluctance had to do with the conversation itself, rather than any of the specifics David had mentioned. She realized, however, that a day does come when matters such as these must be addressed.

"Let me ask, why is it so important that mom go in number six?"

"She wants to be buried with the baby," he replied, as he leafed through some documents on his desk. After several seconds passed, he realized that an awkward silence had engulfed the room, causing him to look up at Wendy.

She was leaning forward in her chair, looking intently at her father. "The baby? What baby?"

"Well, your sister, of course."

Wendy said nothing for some time as she looked into David's face. "You never told me I had a sister."

David was taken aback by his daughter's statement. He leaned forward, his elbows resting on the desk. "What do you mean? Of course we did."

"No, you didn't. You never told me."

The old man's eyebrows rose on his forehead in surprise. *We did tell her, **didn't we?** Surely Elaine must have told her at some point,* he thought to himself.

"I'm sure we must have mentioned it from time to time."

Wendy took a deep breath as she turned from him in frustration.

She then looked back at him and repeated, in as matter-of-fact tone as she could muster, that she had never been told of a sister. "Dad, you never told me about a sister. Mom never told me about her, either. No one mentioned it to me, ever."

David took a deep breath of his own, and sat back in the chair. He gazed down at his desk, contemplatively. "It was a very difficult thing, what happened. It was difficult for both of us, your mother and I. She was our first child. She only lived about ten minutes. I guess we never did talk about it much."

This acknowledgment was followed by a long silence.

"I'm sorry, Dad," she offered in a sympathetic tone, breaking the silence.

He continued looking down at the desk. "Sometimes I wonder what would have become of her. What role she would have played in this life." His voice was tinged with sadness. Wendy looked at her father's sad face as he continued looking at the table, seemingly unable to bring himself back to the moment.

"Dad...dad...look at me," she pleaded. After a few moments, his eyes rose to meet hers. "She has played a role in this life, dad...in my life. More than you know."

Nicole

Nicole, eleven years of age, walked slowly and haphazardly through the woods. She did not leave the path itself, but swayed from one side to the other instead of in a straight line.

She was alone, as far as she knew. It was not a thick woods, the trees were spread out. There were a few bushes, and no bugs. She'd been there for ten minutes, and seemed to have become disoriented. She was not lost, she'd been to this location before. Somehow, this time was different.

It was early October and cool. The sky was clear. She came to a place where the sunlight glittered through the leaves, appearing and disappearing as the wind manipulated the trees. She felt that something was reaching down to embrace her, but wouldn't fully do so just yet. She felt warmth.

She trudged on and came to a clearing. She lay down in the grass, flat on her back. Her eyes closed, she mouthed words but no sound came out. No lip reader in the world could have interpreted.

She moved past the clearing, back into the trees. Doubt, suddenly. Why? She didn't know. Sudden cloud cover, sudden darkness. The cool air was now bordering on cold. The woods were getting thicker, the path narrower. Nicole's senses sharpened.

She stopped suddenly. A fox stood before her in the path. One of its ears were clearly visible, the other turned so that it looked like a thin reed projecting from its head.

A sudden rustling sound to Nicole's right. Her attention was instantly drawn from the fox in the sound's direction. A strange creature, three times her size. Nicole heard an ominous breathing sound, even though the creature appeared utterly motionless. It just stared at her-directly into her eyes. Its eyes became extremely bright, and rotated like kaleidoscopes in their sockets. Its face was so covered by its own overgrown hair that its features, aside from the eyes, were indecipherable. The same was true for the rest of its body, which seemed to lean forward, ready to pounce at any moment.

Nicole stood motionless, staring back at the creature. Her lips began silently mouthing indiscernible words again. This went on for some time. Slowly, the creature began fading. Finally, it disappeared completely.

Nicole, breathing deeply, turned her attention back to the path. The fox was gone, she did not know where it went. She noticed a large pool of white puss a few feet before her, and she sidestepped it. She walked slowly but steadily.

The woods thinned out again. The clouds departed and the sun sparkled again through the swaying leaves. A short time later, she exited the woods and entered the town green. She came to rest in a gazebo, relaxed. Nicole inhaled deeply, her brown hair blown back by the wind.

About the Author

Neil D. Desmond was born in Boston and has lived in Vermont for twenty years. He has a daughter who lives in Massachusetts. His mother is an artist and his uncle is a published poet. Mr. Desmond enjoys creative writing, traveling, as well as watching his share of independent and foreign language films.

Made in the USA
Middletown, DE
16 February 2019